"In *Ever After*, Andrew Ramer weaves his beautiful prose and fanciful imagination with startling concrete details to convince readers their previous knowledge about the lives of beloved authors was inaccurate. His telling of their stories is instead the accurate one. He allows these authors to live longer, more fulfilling lives. *Ever After* is a delightful, engaging read."

—**MIRIAM RUTH BLACK**, author of *Shayna*

"In each of these charming counterfactual biographies, chance extends the life of a famous writer of homophilic inclination. Andrew Ramer taps his many skills—poet, novelist, seer, chronicler of queer culture—to imagine his subjects living openly and enjoying plausible, pleasurable second acts. They write books that we, alas, will never read. But these tales, delightful in their domestic simplicity, are here to remind us that what we long for could be just around the corner."

—**JONATHAN LERNER**, author of
Swords in the Hands of Children

"The Russian writer Yevgeny Zamayatin compared each person to a novel: 'Until the very last page, you don't know how it will end. Otherwise it wouldn't be worth reading.' In *Ever After*, Andrew Ramer provides a final twist to some of the world's greatest authors. In this collection, told with wit and compassion, Ramer imagines new chapters in these writers' lives—and, in so doing, invites us to consider how we, too, might reimagine ours."

—**ANDREW LAWLER**, author of *The Secret Token*

"What if the past had been a little different? Andrew Ramer is the master of mythologizing the human story. What an imaginative and insightful way to consider how arbitrary, evanescent and changeable our ideas of reality are! What if all those stories about unhappy homosexuals had turned out happily ever after instead? *Ever After* offers over ten such alternative stories. Seeing how things could have been different gives us hope they still might be different. And that's what brings it about."

—TOBY JOHNSON, author of *Gay Perspective*

"It seems like Andrew Ramer is doing something delightfully simple here: Imaging other, queer life trajectories for some of our most beloved writers. In reality, he's doing something delightfully subversive as well. He's telling us that other, more just and juicy worlds are possible, and that we can imagine our way into those worlds if we have but a smidgeon of the creativity Ramer brings to these stories."

—SHERI HOSTETLER, author of
So We and Our Children May Live

"*Ever After* takes readers on a pilgrimage through the imagined late lives of authors they have surly cherished throughout their reading journeys. Indeed, the imagined lives and oeuvres reveal aspects and nuances about the authors' inner lives that enrich us as readers, as long as we bear in mind that just because something didn't happen, doesn't mean it isn't true."

—RACHEL BIALE, author of *Lost and Found*

"Queer lives are often thwarted. What might we be if being fully authentic was not denied to us? In *Ever After*, Andrew Ramer retells the lives of authors whose queerness has been suggested, hinted at, implied, and denied and asks what coulda, shoulda, mighta been. His delightful stories have a healing message: embrace who you are and tomorrow can come true."

—**WILL ROSCOE**, author of *Queer Spirits*

"Unexpected eruption of literary scholarship? Sly exercise in historical revisionism? Visionary ode to the healing power of queer love? You will have fun deciding for yourself what Andrew Ramer is up to with *Ever After*."

—**DON SHEWEY**, author of *Daddy Lover God*

"Favorite literary figures who were gone too soon are back—with longer, queerer lives imagined by gifted storyteller Andrew Ramer. In *Ever After*, he opens up new realms of possibility with lifelike, fictional profiles of eleven famous writers. He turns the impossible into delightfully queer reality. Readers who take this journey of queer historical improvisation will feel like found their own happily ever after."

—**KITTREDGE CHERRY**, author of *Art That Dares*

"Andrew Ramer has gifted us with a unique addition to his remarkable body of work. His new book, *Ever After*, takes the reader on a journey of the imagination that has no parallel. Read this slender book and prepare to be enchanted."

—**GAY HENDRICKS**, author of *The Big Leap*

"Andrew Ramer celebrates his personal literary saints by imagining them into queerer shapes, or what they would have been like had their lives reflected queerness they didn't express or perhaps understand. He challenges us to think about the relation between writing and life in new ways, and to recognize that whether or not the geniuses who shaped our culture were queer, there is something inherently queer about genius."

—JOY LADIN, author of *The Future Is Trying to Tell Us Something*

"The transformed lives that Andrew Ramer dreams up for us in *Ever After* are spookily believable. I trust these wild, ingenious histories and the deep truths they convey: that desire is the life force, that our bodies can be answered prayers, that our souls recognize each other and are meant to touch."

—JOAN LARKIN, author of *My Body*

Ever After

Books by Andrew Ramer

From Wipf and Stock:
> *Texting with Angels*
> *Fragments of the Brooklyn Talmud*
> *Deathless*
> *Torah Told Different*
> *Queering the Text*
> *Revelations for a New Millennium*
> *Two Flutes Playing*
> *Two Hearts Dancing*
> *The Spiritual Dimensions of Healing Addictions &*
> *Further Dimensions of Healing Addictions—*
>> with Donna Cunningham

And:
> *Ask Your Angels*—with Alma Daniel and Timothy Wyllie
> *Angel Answers*

Ever After

The Extended Lives and Work
of Eleven Famous Writers

Andrew Ramer

RESOURCE *Publications* · Eugene, Oregon

EVER AFTER
The Extended Lives and Work of Eleven Famous Writers

Resource Publications
An Imprint of Wipf and Stock Publishers
199 W. 8th Ave., Suite 3
Eugene, OR 97401

www.wipfandstock.com

PAPERBACK ISBN: 978-1-6667-7158-9
HARDCOVER ISBN: 978-1-6667-7159-6
EBOOK ISBN: 978-1-6667-7160-2

04/26/23

In memory of—
Irmgard Baum, Richard Eisenberg,
Joseph McKay, Gerard Rizza, Chris Cox,
and Lynne Reynolds

Contents

Variations on a Dream

FOR SOME REASON, PAINTERS are allowed to paint the same scene over and over again. Think: Monet's cathedral variations, and Georgia O'Keeffe's flowers. And musicians can explore variations on the same theme, over and over again, too. Writers, however, are not supposed to repeat themselves. I don't know why. So be warned—there is only one plot here, told ten times, about eleven of my favorite Western writers, one other figure from history, and eight people introduced to me by my muses. (Please note that the background for each author's life is historically accurate, more or less—until the moment I start to tinker with it.)

Here's a brief history of this book. On the night of May 29th 1985 I dreamed that I was at a garage sale and came upon a boxed-set of Jane Austen's collected works. It had exactly the same bindings and covers as the one my mother owned, only it was twice as wide—because it included poems, novels, essays, and plays that Austen wrote after she moved to America, where she died some years later, of old age.

This book has other roots. Virginia Woolf writing about Shakespeare's sister Judith. My fascination with stories where the South won the War Between the States and the Nazis won the Second World War. Air pollution? We could be living without it—if we'd made other choices than to be dependent upon automobiles. Solar energy? What would the world be like if Ronald Reagan hadn't been elected president, or was—but left the solar panels on the White House roof that Jimmy Carter installed?

True stories are a co-parent of this book as well. My second mother Irmgard Baum and her mother and brother got out of Germany on the last (sealed) train upon which Jews could leave the country. She was sixteen, lost most of her family and friends in the Holocaust, and lived a very difficult life, riding long waves of depression. Utterly single for forty years, at age eighty, after much resistance, she accepted a dinner invitation from a charming widower in her building who I would have gone out with myself—and told her so. They fell in love, and the last three years of her life with Dr. Richard Eisenberg cast a luminous light on her entire life, changing it backwards and forwards, which changed my life too.

I had my Austen dream in 1985, and it continued to echo in my head. On August 10, 2012 I wrote in my journal:

> Instead of dying, Alexander the Great lives to conquer much of the known world, and creates a unified empire that endures for hundreds of years, sharing his throne with a beloved companion, the Hephaestion of his youth.

I went on to imagine a tale about Jane Austen that emerged from and played with my dream, and also imagined stories about George Elliot, Marcel Proust, Oscar Wilde, and about Virginia Woolf and her partner Doris Lefkowitz, who I'd mentioned in "Mincha," a story in *Queering the Text*, published in 2010, about the first trans winner of a Nobel Prize in literature. My journal notes also included a reference to "Milk and Cookies," a still-unpublished story:

> Instead of being murdered, Harvey Milk went on to become the governor of California, lost his bid for the presidency, created a global foundation for gay youth, and ended up working for the UN.

The first story I actually wrote for this book, during the summer of 2015, is the one about George Elliot. Then I wrote the story about Austen, and continued on, never getting to Alexander the Great, or to another imagined tale that haunts me now, during the autumn of 2022, as I read about the continuing invasion of Ukraine, where all of my grandparents came from:

> Emperor Nicholas II and Empress Alexandra of Russia have another son, also named Nicholas, who isn't (like Alexei, their only son in this reality) a hemophiliac. When his father is forced to abdicate he succeeds him, as Nicholas

VARIATIONS ON A DREAM

III, and his long life and reign change the course of Russian history. No USSR.

And, naturally—he's gay.

I want an invented truth.

CLARICE LISPECTOR, *ÁGUA VIVA*

Jane Austen in Boston

SHE SELDOM SPOKE OF it, or mentioned it in her extensive correspondence. In fact she only wrote about it once at length, a decade later, in her diary:

> There was a moment in the darkness when it seemed as if the fragile little boat of me was going to be swept out to sea, just as the doctor and my beloved sister feared. But then, to everyone's surprise and delight, including my own—although not immediately, for there was something comforting about that vast expanse of welcoming sea—I was caught up tenderly in a slow warm unexpected current that carried me back safely toward dry land.

Twenty years later Austen would expand upon that passage, giving her own near-death experience to Harriet Dawson, the protagonist of her final novel, *Toward Morning*, which was published in 1855, a year before her death.

What would we say of Jane Austen if she had in fact died in 1817, of a disease which to this day remains a mystery. Some say it was a recurrence of typhus which she'd had as a child. On the rare occasions when she did refer to it, she always called that terrifying episode either "Bile" or "Rheumatism," downplaying its significance. Had she perished, while we would have her comic juvenilia and the four marvelous works published in England before her illness—think of all that we would have to live without—seven more novels, three poetry collections, six plays, three volumes of essays, commentaries, and book reviews, plus her extensive journals, which make her one of the most loved writers in all of English literature. These writings we owe to the Hippocratic wisdom of Doctor Eugene Bridges, whose "magic potion," as Austen's sister Cassandra called it, remains equally a mystery, as a fire some years later, long after Miss Austen had moved to America, destroyed all of his papers.

A brief biography should suffice. Jane Austen was born in 1775 to parents in the lower ranks of the landed gentry. Her family was large—six brothers and an older sister, Cassandra. Her father was a rector whose career had some notable ups and down, but he provided as well as he could for his children, and to the best of his ability nurtured the talents of his daughters, Jane a writer and Cassandra an artist. All of this, plus her only courtship—which ended badly—and a later proposal of marriage that Jane accepted and then declined a day later, are the background for her sharp wit and incisive commentaries on the world around her.

As marriage was the central theme of her English novels, death became the central theme of her American ones. We might trace the arc of her work from the first line of her most popular English novel, *Pride and Prejudice:*

> It is a truth universally acknowledged, that a single man in possession of a good fortune, must be in want of a wife—

to the closing line of her most autobiographical and final American novel, *Toward Morning:*

> There was a moment, Harriet thought, when all that had gone before, the journey, the waves, the dark rocky shore, continued to call her, down and down—but. . . . . not quite yet.

Literary scholars tend to distinguish between two patterns in the world of great writers. Some burst upon the scene fully formed, like Athena from the head of her father, while others, like Isis, come upon their genius gradually, growing step by small step. Jane Austen is a curious combination of both of those patterns; a young comic genius and a somber accomplished wordsmith later in life. Not that there aren't a few earlier suggestions of the direction she might be heading in. For example, here is a comment she made in 1814 in a letter to her niece Anna:

At the bottom of Kingsdown Hill we met a gentleman in a buggy, who, on minute examination, turned out to be Dr. Hall—and Dr. Hall in such very deep mourning that either his mother, his wife, or himself must be dead.

More surprising than the metamorphosis of Józef Korzeniowski into Joseph Konrad was the metamorphosis of one Jane Austen into the other, with literally an ocean between them. We all know the story. Some months after her recovery from that mysterious near-fatal illness, Jane and her sister Cassandra traveled to Bath, where they had lived before, so that Jane could convalesce and take the waters in one of the city's many spas. It was there that the first Jane Austen met Veronica Ledley, the spinster daughter of an American sea captain, Thomas Ledley, who had brought his ailing daughter to Bath to convalesce. Austen was forty-two, Ledley was thirty-five, and how we wish that an author whose collected works fill twenty-three volumes, would have recorded some of what those two no-longer-young women said to each other as they regained their health. We do know Cassandra's dismay when her younger and slowly rejuvenating sister announced her intention to move to Boston with her new friend. Cassandra felt abandoned, betrayed, and yet somewhat in awe of her beloved sister. For some of us, serious illness puts an end to our lives, even if we recover; and for others, serious illness is an invitation to embrace life. And so, in April of 1818, Jane Austen and Veronica Ledley crossed a choppy Atlantic Ocean together, and set up housekeeping on Beacon Hill, in a home that they would share for the rest of Austen's life.

Historians believe that the expression "Boston Marriage," which describes two women of independent means who set up housekeeping, was first used to talk about Austen and Ledley. And how we 21st century voyeurs want to know the secret that both of them took to their graves—"Were they lovers?" And yet, in a time such as ours that values such revelations, and which places such emphasis upon love and marriage, now in this and other countries extended to same-sex couples—the question that we really have to ask ourselves is—"Does it matter?" All that we may need to know is that a Miss Ledley invited a Miss Austen to share her life, and in that sense Veronica Ledley is responsible for the birth of the second Jane Austen, the American one.

Few of us today read her comic English novels. Virginia Woolf wrote accurately that the second Miss Austen, the American one, was the forerunner of both Henry James and Marcel Proust, through her dark American novels of disappointment, poverty, and oppression. We know that as a youth James's family moved to Boston, where they were entertained on several occasions in the years after Austen's death by the elderly Miss Ledley, and we know that as a younger man Proust saw productions of several of Austen's American plays including, *The Elder Sister* and *After the Fire*. Today we pore over her novels, poems, plays, and the many letters that she and her sister exchanged, sometimes daily, and we picture her wandering the streets of 19th Century Boston, her arm slipped through that of Miss Ledley, as we see in the only known photographic image of the two of them, a daguerreotype taken in a studio in 1850. Two women of a certain age are staring into the camera, frozen for a moment, their upper bodies apart and their voluminous skirts pressed together. And we can hear them laughing at their little private joke, found in one of Austen's journals, but only made public after her death:

> It is a truth universally ignored, everywhere but here, for some strange reason, that Austen and Boston—do not rhyme.

Of course we wonder, of those early novels about marriage, her one failed courtship, and the marriage offer returned a day after it was delivered—if this was a case of, "Me thinks the lady doth protest too much." And we ask ourselves—"Was this the case of a deeply closeted woman, who at an age when most of her contemporaries were settling into their new roles as grandparents—chose to cross a dark choppy ocean in order to come out?" But in the end all that we can say, even reading through the five volumes of her journal, is that a small bright woman of letters who reinvented herself midway through life, spent the last thirty-eight years of that life growing happier and happier, gazing out of her study window on Beacon Hill toward the harbor, an infallible social witness, writing dark psychological works decades before Freud was advancing his theories, those late works of hers prominently displayed on the shelves behind his desk.

Deep in the Woods

NARRATIVES AND COUNTER-NARRATIVES DANCE. What is and what could have been, spiral and twine, inviting us to consider what yet might be. In a time of increasing global degradation we wish we'd paid more careful attention to the writings of naturalist Henry David Thoreau, going back for inspiration to *Walden, A Year in the Forest,* and his beautiful Minnesota essays, *Under a Rose Moon.* In a nation grown increasingly Buddhist we return again to Thoreau, seeing him and his Transcendentalist writings as a bridge between West and East, between communal and contemplative. Grappling with how to live in the world, how to live with ourselves, and how to create a just system of government that balances both of those concerns, it's Thoreau the abolitionist and social reformer who is our teacher, in *Civil Disobedience, Life Without Principle,* and the manuscript he left unfinished at his death in 1887, *In the Image of Justice.* There he plays with Biblical and Native American themes to establish a secular theology of right relationships with self, others, and the world. And lastly, we owe a huge debt to the elegant stylist whose work continues to inspire writers and thinkers in this country and around the world, which is ironic for the work of a small town boy whose best days were spent in two different cabins, so well documented in *Walden* and in his final masterpiece, *Deep in the Woods.*

Born in 1817, the third of four children, Thoreau entered Harvard College at age sixteen, graduated and went on to tutor and teach until a canoe trip when he was twenty-two awakened him to his true calling—to become a student and poet of nature. For some years Thoreau lived with his mentor Ralph Waldo Emerson and his family, working as a handyman, editor, baby sitter, and contributor to Emerson's Transcendentalist magazine, *The Dial.* In

1847 he began the solo adventure he is famous for—living for two years, two months, and two days in a cabin on Emerson's property on Walden Pond. While some have quibbled about how solo that time actually was, his experience there and his book about it are foundational for our modern culture.

It's always a challenge to look back at someone's life from the present. Words, concepts, ideas and identities that seem obvious and clear to us today cannot always be translated backwards. Most historians and even his contemporaries viewed Thoreau's character in his younger years as being cold. Today we might call him repressed, wondering if he was gender-queer, bisexual, or simply gay. We know that he was devastated when Ellen Sewall rejected his marriage proposal, and we know about his attachment to Tom Fowler, the guide who he chose for his trip to the Maine woods and later to Aleck Therien the Canadian woodchopper who visited him at Walden Pond. As to the warm letters he wrote to Emerson's wife's older widowed sister Lucy, we can see them as both love letters and the missives of a gay man to his best straight woman friend. And how do we factor loss into the workings of a person's heart? Within weeks of each other, in January of 1842, both Thoreau's older brother John and Emerson's young son Waldo died. Did that add another layer of contraction to his already restrained temperament? That we cannot know, but what we can be sure of is that for much of his adult life Thoreau loved best words and the natural world, both of them equally.

In 1835 Thoreau contracted what was then called consumption, today tuberculosis, and he suffered with ill health for many years afterward. (And what does that do to someone's heart—or their libido?) In those days one cure for consumption was a change of climate, and in 1861 Thoreau's doctor suggested a trip to Minnesota. He set out in May of that year with a traveling companion, Horace Mann Jr., the seventeen-year-old son of friends and an aspiring naturalist. They took a series of trains out West and had numerous adventures exploring the region, which both richly documented, in addition to collecting specimens. During the trip Mann wrote back to his family that Thoreau seemed much improved by their time on land and water. They had planned to return home to Massachusetts by steamship and then train and spent their last few nights in St. Paul at the home of a fellow naturalist, the Prussian-Jewish poet Friedrich Baum. On their second night there Baum invited six other writers and naturalists to a gathering, among them a man named Peter White Crane, an Ojibwe Native who'd been raised in his family's village and then educated by missionaries at a local French Jesuit academy.

Would that someone had been there with a cellphone to discreetly video the encounter of the man Thoreau simply called White Crane, the English translation of his Ojibwe name. We know little of his background and, ever discreet himself, Thoreau preserved little in his journal or other writings. A single photograph taken of the two of them a few years later reveals a gaunt face and a round face, and two sets of intense eyes, one pair light and the other dark. We know that Thoreau was three years older than White Crane, who as a European-educated Native lived in multiple worlds. He spoken fluent English and French in addition to his mother tongue, and although he stood at the center of Baum's parlor on that warm spring evening in 1861 dressed as a proper American gentleman, in his own community White Crane would have been called in the parlance of the time a "berdache," from a French slang word for a boy prostitute that is itself derived from an Arabic word for a slave boy. Today we would probably speak of White Crane as being a third-gender or Two-Spirit person, a man who in his own community dressed in mixed male and female garb, served a role as ritual leader and shaman, and most often had intimate relationships with other men. But none of that was revealed that night—at least not verbally. What we know from Thoreau's journal is that two things happened by the glow of several recently invented kerosene lamps—that each tall slim and no longer young man felt a deep sense of kinship with the other—and that the two began a correspondence when Thoreau and Mann returned home to Concord in July. Their surviving letters are both intimate and clear, both coded and overt in the romantic language of the time, which permitted two men to long for each other in ways that would be culturally forbidden a generation later.

Thoreau's family and friends were delighted to welcome home a happier healthier man, but when he announced six months later that he would be moving to St. Paul in the spring—they reacted with shock and horror. We tend to think of Thoreau as a homebody, and he helps us to sustain this image of him, as when he wrote in his journal in 1857 that our favorite books are not by those who have traveled widely but by those who "lived the deepest and been the most at home." In fact, he had traveled a good deal in his home state and region before he made that journey West, and the reason he gave for his move was simple and true—Baum had offered to house him and to sponsor his exploration of the flora and fauna of the region, something that he and White Crane continued do to until his death a quarter of a century later.

Thoreau deliberately arrived in St. Paul on the first anniversary of his meeting White Crane, who was waiting for him at the train station carrying a spray of flowers. Of the man who earlier had written both, "The mass of men lead lives of quiet desperation" and "The language of friendship is not words but meaning" we do know this, that desperation vanished during the time he shared with his beloved White Crane, who outlived him by only three years. The work they did together was monumental—a vast compendium of the plants, trees, animals and birds of the region, arranged season by season, that biologists still make use of today. While Thoreau was working on his poetry and essays White Crane was doing ethnographic studies of his own people, and a photograph taken of him in Ojibwe garb shows a still-handsome man in his late fifties wearing a long fringed shawl covered with opulent floral beadwork that he designed and sewed himself. And then there are Thoreau's poems. Years earlier he had gone to meet Walt Whitman, and their visit left each man both impressed and wary of the other. Thoreau's letters to Whitman from St. Paul did not survive, but we know from Whitman's letters to Thoreau, which did, that Thoreau had written something to Whitman that shifted their relationship. We can only speculate that he himself addressed his former reticence, and wrote of the ways in which his relationship to White Crane had changed him—because their letters grew increasingly warmer and more intimate, and we have Whitman's lovely poem, "My Friend's New Journey," penned upon hearing of Thoreau's death.

For several years Thoreau lived with Baum and his family, a curious repeat of his life with the Emersons, and then in 1866, a year after the Civil War had reached its brutal end, Thoreau and White Crane purchased land on the shores of Lake Superior, where they built a two-room cabin, which became their home till Thoreau's death. The cabin was near White Crane's village, we know that the two spent time there, and from his writings we can see the ways in which a society that honored difference welcomed and honored them. Reviving his old skills, Whitman taught English classes there, and White Crane taught him Ojibwe, which he picked up quickly, although White Crane always teased him about his terrible accent. During those years White Crane wrote the book he's best known for, *Living on Holy Ground,* that study of what has come to be called ecology, and which remains a basic handbook for anyone who wants to live in harmony with the Earth. His political work in St. Paul established a level of Native inclusion that spread to other states, and Minnesota was the first state in the Union to require that all of its students learn one Native language. We are also blessed to have Thoreau's glorious book about their time together, *Deep in the Woods,* published five years before his death—into which he was midwifed by White Crane. Thoreau's remains were interred in White Crane's village, and in that same plot of land he himself was interred three years later. The work of these two men lives on, and to this day students around the world buy Thoreau's two classics, *Walden Pond* and *Deep in the Woods,* bound together in one thick volume. I still have the copy I bought in college, their only photograph on its cover, its pages yellow and crumbling on the rare occasions that I open it, sitting beside the newer edition that I keep going back to.

The Greatest Novel in the Western Canon

IN 2011 THE *NEW York Times* ran a series by Anthony Tommasini on the top ten classical music composers. His ranking, with Bach at the top, and the hundreds of responses he received, revealed a vast range of opinions as to who should have been included— chiefly women and non-Western composers—many of those comments written in heated tones usually found when talking about sports, politics, religion, the environment, and war. How lucky to represent a different art, one where intense conflict does not exist, for in the world of Western literature there are no dissenting voices. All agree that English author George Eliot's final novel, *The Deronda Sisters,* published in 1885, is a masterpiece that tingles with life and exceeds by good measure the cherished works of Western authors Cervantes, Austen, Tolstoy, Dostoevsky, Dickens, Twain, Joyce, Proust, Woolf, Lispector, and countless others both before and after her.

Born in 1819, Mary Ann Evans began her writing career as a translator of Spinoza and as an essayist. Only in her thirties did she begin to write fiction and poetry, published under the name George Eliot, beginning with *Adam Bede,* published in 1859, and continuing on to *Middlemarch,* published in 1871 and *Daniel Deronda,* published in 1876.

From her later diary notes we can trace the slow development of her masterpiece. After the publication of *Daniel Deronda,* with its disappointing sales, Eliot turned back to non-fiction, eventually completing three collections of essays. The death two years later of her longtime companion George Lewes, and then her unexpected marriage to John Cross two years after that, were major trials. His death by drowning while they were honeymooning left Eliot a devastated woman who struggled back to England where her own health collapsed. For the next two years, well cared for, she hovered at death's door, and it's from out of that long dark period in her life that she crafted the Western world's greatest work of fiction.

What amazes a reader who comes to her earlier novel *Middlemarch* is its passion. And yet many agree that the work is flawed, the characters too true to type, and the intertwined plots artificial and unbalanced. Her next book, *Daniel Deronda,* with better pacing and somewhat fuller characters, heartful as it is, lacks the vitality that infuses *Middlemarch,* and many critics have seen its two intertwined stories as imperfectly matched, almost as if the book were two novels spliced together, some favoring one story and some the other. What became *The Deronda Sisters* did not begin as a sequel, but as a short story Eliot wrote during her long convalescence, closely patterned on the three daughters of a titled family she and Lewes had known, the eldest daughter of which had taken her own life. The story began as a tribute to that young woman, and was also a contained way for Eliot to work through layers of her own grief. There is no mention of the Derondas in that draft or in the next one, written three years after Cross's death, as she was slowly returning to health. It's only in her third revision that Eliot returned to the story of Daniel and Mirah Deronda, giving them the three daughters who are the main characters of her unfolding story.

Sequels are common today, but they were rare in Eliot's time. Some have seen this continuing story of the Deronda clan as a lifeline that Eliot cast out for herself, an act of triumph and survival, in a book that is darker than any of her previous works, and at the same time far more luminous and transcendent. As in her two previous books, there are interwoven plots, but in *The Deronda Sisters* Eliot perfected her craft. The stories of the three sisters are equal in power, and not just the writing but the subject matter raised her work to a level of high genius. In *Daniel Deronda* Eliot tackled the Jewish Question, at a time when almost no Jewish writers were approaching it, and her exploration of Jewishness continued in the sequel, all the more remarkable from an author who was not herself Jewish. There we meet the eldest sister Sylvia, whose conversion and marriage to an Anglican peer brought her both joy and loss. Then we meet middle sister Tamara, who struggled with the religious heritage she inherited, seeking a place for a woman teacher, a woman rabbi, a century too soon. Eliot's courage and creativity is revealed in the story of their youngest sister Clara, a musician, charting the slow awakening of her love for another woman, something which few writers were willing to visit at that time, and none of them in print.

It's Clara we meet first, in the book's opening lines:

> Turning in her chair, she caught through the high casement window a glimpse of the moon, first a sliver, then a shining disc, topaz, as it began its slow rise, up over the hills and into the black and starless sky. Clara put her embroidery down on the table before her, gathered her skirts about her, and crossed to that open window, there to stand in the warming glow of that still September night.

The moon becomes Clara's guide, her symbol, and Eliot titled the first complete draft of the book *Topaz Moon,* establishing Clara as the central character. But she soon realized that Clara's story could not stand without those of her sisters—Sylvia, a painter, wife and mother, who fully embraces life in a new world, and Tamara who probes and writes so brilliantly, and succeeds as a writer much as Eliot had, not without losses and wounds in both of their lives. Unlike her previous novels, in *The Deronda Sisters* there are no subplots; instead, each sister's narrative is of equal weight. And of course, each reader has their favorite sister. My brother Richard, a gifted pianist, prefers Tamara the writer. My sister Lynne, a talented poet, would nominate Sylvia the painter as the most important. For me the central character is Clara, the composer, whose art reveals the deep wellsprings of her people, and whose requited passion for the visiting German-Jewish violinist Natalie Gruenwald was a clarion call for liberation long before others were writing about same-sex love.

Certainly Eliot's survival of illness, loss, abandonment, betrayal, near death, and eventual rebirth, infuse the book with her irrepressible vitality. And in the curious way in which life doesn't just imitate art but is invoked by it, Eliot in her journal comments that:

> *Writing* Middlemarch *prepared me to embrace the many faces of love, and writing* Daniel Deronda *paved the way for me to continue that journey.*

While scholars have written about the same-sex attractions and occasional transgender leanings of some of Eliot's characters, unlike with Austen, there is no debate as to the precise nature of Eliot's connection with Madeline Fromberg Cohen. Their companionship began with Cohen writing Eliot a fan letter about her work, continued till Eliot's death in 1883, at the age of seventy-four, certainly influenced her most famous book—and Eliot mentions in her journal the delightful irony of the woman with a man's name being courted by another woman. The two shared a large flat in Paris, which Cohen inherited from her industrialist father, and it was there that Eliot wrote four drafts of what became *The Deronda Sisters*, reading each draft to Cohen. From Eliot's penciled notes in the margins of those drafts, we can see how Cohen's suggestions were incorporated, in a way that is none the less pure Eliot.

Critics looking at these three novels, *Middlemarch, Daniel Deronda,* and *The Deronda Sisters,* chart with clear steps Eliot's march from great to greater to greatness. No summary of a novel can ever do it justice, and many who have attempted to write about her last book have taken hands off their keyboards in despair. As if she were a sybil, a prophetess, Eliot left us a luminous book that prefigures films in its vividness: the cuts from scene to scene, the eerily "modern" sound and feel of her words, have nothing Victorian about them. Rich with language that at times becomes pure music, her three sisters dance separately and together through life, with an intensity that enlivens and uplifts. Proust aspired toward Eliot's vibrancy, Woolf at times imitated it, but to date no other writer has come close to her exalted throne, although comparisons are often made to Dostoevsky's three brothers and Chekhov's three sisters. As a writer myself, I can almost envy Mr. Tomassini his musical challenge. His landscape has many shining peaks; we book lovers gaze sun-blind toward one vast mountain top, easy to point out on the horizon. And now all book lovers can rejoice at the unmatched blessing of being able to read the digital edition of George Eliot's *The Deronda Sisters*—with all of her draft notes hypertexted, for the very first time. You can read it in bed, on an airplane, at the kitchen table, beneath a beach umbrella, and now backlit, in the words that Eliot gave to Clara, sitting at her writing table, staring out a closed window, into:

> . . . a cold starless night, with a topaz moon shining, a
> pearly one, an obscured one, or none at all.

At the Station

IN 1862, SHORTLY BEFORE their wedding, in the spirit of honesty with which he hoped to live out his married life, thirty-four year old Count Leo Tolstoy gave his fiancée Sophia Behrs his journal to read. Sixteen years his junior, she was horrified by his sexual exploits with women who were his serfs, and by his occasional attraction to other men. And so, with hope and horror they began a shared life that brought thirteen children into the world, eight of whom survived. Never an easy marriage, Tolstoy moved from sexual obsession to celibacy, each straining the relationship in different ways, and as the two grew older it deteriorated more and more, until—the inversion of a child running away from home—in the early hours of October 28, 1910—it was the patriarch, the father, who quietly said goodbye to his favorite daughter Alexandra and slipped out of the house in which everyone else was sleeping, accompanied only by his doctor, Dushan Makovitsky.

We all know the story of their escape, and the strategies they took to avoid being followed, as the most famous author in the Russian Empire, the creator of *War and Peace, Anna Karenina,* and volumes of essays and other works of fiction, in running away from what he called a prison, stumbled instead into a garden, so very very late in life. He was eighty-two.

Tolstoy and Makovitsky secretly made their way to the convent where Tolstoy's sister Maria had lived for twenty years. In the morning they slipped away again, intent upon taking the train from the small station at Shchekino to Kozelsk Station in Kaluga Province. It was October 31, and after all of their escapades, the forest path they had to take to the station was challenging for anyone, especially a man in his early eighties, and Tolstoy was limping, exhausted.

They missed the train.

The tiny station is long gone. A marker on a post there is all that tells a tourist of what happened. Tolstoy and his doctor collapsed on a bench as the train vanished in the distance, leaving behind a trail of undulating steam. There were very few people on the tiny platform, a few servants and a distinguished older man who had a small estate nearby, there to see his younger brother off, who had been visiting from Saint Petersburg. The man was an anomaly in the region, a Turkish lawyer who had inherited his estate from a Russian client he'd kept out of jail, who'd been blackmailed by a foreign ambassador. Waving till the train was out of sight, Yusuf Kaya turned back toward his waiting carriage and then noticed, sitting on a low wooden bench, the panting bearded writer known around the world.

At seventy-one Yusuf Kaya was a tall, still-vigorous man who strode up to the count, bowed, introduced himself, and asked if he could be of service. It was Dr. Makovitsky who explained their situation, to which Kaya invited them to return home with him. Tolstoy sent off a telegram to his beloved daughter Alexandra, telling her of his progress, but not telling her where he was going, and the three men rode off in the waiting carriage, to the small but very comfortable home where Tolstoy would spend the rest of his life.

To many this turn of events is unexpected. Younger people are horrified that two old men might fall in love. Others are horrified that this man who had lived through a spiritual conversion, been excommunicated by the Orthodox Church, and then become a hero to millions around the world for his teachings on faith, equality, and pacifism, could fall in love so late in life. Even stranger than that was that this new relationship—with another man—turned two fierce rivals, Tolstoy's wife and his chief disciple Vladimir Chertkov, into the best of friends, as they desperately struggled to get the count to return home. For Sonya Tolstoy, who had once accused her husband of being Chertkov's lover, this was a bitter ironic pill to swallow, and for Chertkov, to be replaced in the count's affections in an even deeper way, was an equally bitter pill. Poor Alexandra did her best to make peace between the various factions, but as Leo had revealed all to his fiancée, he did the same to his daughter, who moved from dismay to gratitude, when she joined her father at Kaya's estate and saw how happy he was, happy in a way that she had never seen before—although for quite some time no one else knew what the true relationship was between the two men, other than host and permanent guest. And in that generous generative house of love, Alexandra and her father's physician grew closer and closer themselves, and a year later they were married in the garden, with only her father and Kaya as witnesses.

But we ought not to be surprised by this particular flowering of love late in life. Tolstoy left us many clues as to his feelings about other men, and not just in his journal. Looking at *War and Peace,* for example, we find hints early on of the author's inclinations—in his description of the way that Pierre was drawn to Boris, how Tushin looked at another man, we also meet a man with a woman's name, several instances of cross-dressing, and, in Tolstoy's at-times tender descriptions of some of his male characters, we find a gateway into the mind, heart, and body of a man who was seeking something, without perhaps knowing what it was himself—till it appeared in the guise of a kind slightly younger foreign gentlemen who had copies of all of his books in his library, in several different languages.

Some of Tolstoy's fans were outraged by this taking up residence with a Muslim, even if they never knew the depth of their connection. So please consider this, from a letter Tolstoy wrote in 1884, some years before their chance encounter:

> *Some liberals and aesthetes—consider me to be mad or weak-minded like Gogol; others—revolutionaries and radicals—consider me to be a mystic and a man who talks too much; the officials consider me to be a malicious revolutionary; the Orthodox consider me to be a devil. I confess that it is hard for me . . . And therefore, please, regard me as a kind of Mohammedan, and all will be fine.*

To this day there are scholars who deny the truth of the relationship between the great Russian novelist and the distinguished Turkish lawyer. Others downplay it, forgetting that long before

Stonewall people were writing and speaking about homosexuality. And let's consider Tolstoy's last marvelous novel, *Alexander in Egypt,* that fantasy about how, instead of dying at age thirty-three, Alexander the Great lived to conquer much of the known world, and created a unified empire with its capital in Alexandria that endured for hundreds of years, sharing his throne with his beloved companion from youth, Hephaestion—which was clearly modeled on his relationship with Yusuf Kaya, his glowing descriptions of Alexander's capital city a tribute to his own beloved daughter.

You know how much I like photographs. Two of my favorites are the one that Kaya, an amateur photographer, took of Tolstoy's writing table in their home, looking out through French doors into a lush garden. And even more I like the one that Alexandra took of Kaya and her father on Tolstoy's eighty-third birthday. The two men are sitting outside in that garden, in high-backed rattan chairs. Tolstoy is dressed as we have come to know him, in a white peasant's shirt, and Kaya is sitting beside him in a Western suit and tie, the tassel of his fez dangling over the side. His head is turned toward Tolstoy's, at an angle, and the great author has one of his large gnarled hands lightly resting on Kaya's, as it sits on the arm of his chair. Tolstoy is looking at the camera, but that hand, that hand which has now lingered there for more than one hundred years, tells us everything.

Think of the arc of a life, a long life. His many years with Sonya, their many children, the wars, the books, the losses, the struggles internal and external. And think of what this means to all of us, as we grow older. Three months before he died, in June of 1913, Tolstoy wrote a short letter of apology to Sonya, acknowledging that both knew their relationship had ended long long before it was over. His letter concludes with:

> *Did I deserve this happiness, so late in life? Does any man deserve anything? I am thinking back to Don Quixote, who said, "Each of us is as God made him, and often much worse." To you my dear Sonya I was often much worse, from the very start. For that I beg your forgiveness, knowing that I do not deserve it. And yet, we had our good*

> times, and brought into the world our wonderful children,
> and as I come now to the end of my days I wish for you
> the joy that I have found—and more—for you have always
> been a better person than I am. Please forgive me.

To Kaya he wrote this, in a card that he gave him on his
seventy-third birthday:

> You my friend have taught me what it means to be both old
> and young, to feel the passion I felt as a young man all over
> again, in a different key, a different tone. As if the music had
> somehow changed from that of my friend Rachmaninoff to
> that of Chopin, perhaps. Thank you, for waking me up and
> slowing me down, all at the same time. There is more in
> your eyes than in all of my novels, and more in your kind
> touch than a thousand mothers could provide.

Tolstoy died on a warm spring day, his lover and his daughter
on either side of his bed. At Tolstoy's request, Kaya took photographs of him afterwards. And also at his request, Alexandra and
her husband remained with Kaya, the two of them continuing
the work that Tolstoy had begun, publishing his books on non-
violence. Tolstoy was buried in Yusuf Kaya's garden, and Kaya was
buried beside him five years later, a year before the Revolution.
Today their joint graves are visited by pilgrims from around the
world, particularly same-sex lovers, who see in the two men a possibility for love, even brief love, that can illuminate the soul. The
two tall stones, side by side, carry words that Tolstoy penned in
English. In his eighty-forth year he was giving Kaya English lessons
every afternoon. On Tolstoy's grave we read: "Dancing Souls;" on
Kaya's grave we read: "Souls Dancing," taken from the last note the
count wrote to the lawyer before he died:

> We are dancing souls, my beautiful Joseph of the Bible, the
> Koran.
>
> We are souls dancing—even if we are now too old to stand.

Ice Skating on the Moon

"UNLIKELY" IS THE WORD used by most biographers and historians to describe their relationship, often prefaced by: "Very, most, highly, extremely, entirely . . ."

Well-published, her work recognized here and abroad, Emma Lazarus was a voracious reader, with a particular writer's voice shaped by its culture, her background, and by the upheavals of her time. She knew the work of the older writer, Emily Dickinson, although very little of her writing had been published, and what was had been highly edited, in order to remove the uniqueness of a voice so *not* shaped by its culture or by her background, edited to mold her words to fit the conventions of the time, conventions that Emma respected and lived by, as a chess player respects the rules, as a flautist honors the musical notes on the page before her.

Yes, Emma knew the myth about this reclusive writer who only wore white, but her words, her daring, her marvelous voice began to haunt Emma, who began to feel that her own voice was being stifled by the attention given to it. She wished she could have written to her mentor and friend, Ralph Waldo Emerson, whose work she knew had influenced that of Miss Dickinson, to ask for his advice, but he had been slipping away for some time and had recently died. Instead, in the midst of making plans for a trip to Europe, where her work was so deeply rooted, she persuaded her older sister Josephine to accompany her to Amherst, Massachusetts, a several day's journey by train and carriage from New York that revealed to the two women a lovely corner of the county they had never before seen.

It was a beautiful spring day in Amherst. The sisters spent the night in a hotel in the center of town, and then asked directions to the writer's home from one of the maids, a more likely source of information, they thought, than the owner or others of the staff. Late in the morning the sisters set out to meet the poet. Emma had agonized—"Should I have written in advance? Should I bring her a gift? One of my books?" In the end Josephine had persuaded her to take a copy of, not her own poems but her translations of the work of Heinrich Heine, which had just been published, although on their short walk there Emma decided not to embarrass the older writer whose work had been so little published, and decided to leave it in her reticule.

An elegant brick house painted ochre and off-white, surrounded by a white fence, with an elegant but slightly awkward cupola, perhaps an afterthought, on the dark roof. A large tree on the lawn. Stately, they decided, stopping. Emma, nervous, to her sister's surprise, wanted to turn away, but the older sister pushed the younger one ahead, telling her that she wanted to walk about the town and would meet up with her for tea back at the hotel.

It was shortly after ten on the morning of Tuesday April 3, 1883 as a woman moving toward her thirty-forth birthday, dressed in burgundy, a light tan cape over her shoulders, her thick dark hair just starting to go gray and wrapped in a braid around her head, climbed the steps from the street, pushed open the gate, walked up the front path, up the stairs, nearly fled, and then took a deep breath and pulled on the bell-ringer.

It was shortly after ten on the morning of Tuesday April 3, 1883 when a woman moving toward her fifty-third birthday, her still-dark ruddy hair parted in the middle and pulled back in a tight bun, heard the doorbell ring and slowly made her way from the parlor to see who was there, wearing a long white shawl over her simple pearly-white dress. As she swung open the door a swarthy younger woman stood before her, looking anxious, who had to clear her voice to say, "Forgive me for troubling you. I'm Miss Lazarus." She'd heard that the poet never left her room. Was this her sister? But a warm smile broke across the poet's lively face as she reached out a hand and said, "Good morning. I'm Miss Emily Dickinson, and if you are Miss Lazarus the poet, then I am most delighted to meet you."

Three hours later Emma remembered her sister. The two po-
ets had been talking without a break since her arrival, over their
work and over the eventually-given Heine translations, and they
declined an offer for lunch from both a servant and then the poet's
sister Lavinia, who stuck her head in, curious to find out about
the animated conversation going on in the parlor. Informing Miss
Dickinson of her promise to meet her own sister for tea, Emma
Lazarus began to excuse herself, but her hostess would not hear of it
until she'd elicited a promise for the sisters to join her and her own
sister for dinner that evening, which they did, returning to Manhattan the next day, after a very brief visit the following morning.

Today we can read the volume of letters those two so very
different women sent back and forth for the next few months, si-
lenced only in August when instead of her usual summer with the
rest of the large Lazarus clan in Newport, Rhode Island, Emma
made her second visit to Amherst, by herself. We know that after a
single night in the hotel in town, at Emily's invitation, she moved
into the Dickinson home, where she remained for a week. Shortly
afterwards Emma Lazarus went off on her long-planned trip to
Europe, the letters continued, and when she returned to America
it was to the Dickinson house, where she wrote one of her most
noted poems, "The New Colossus," to raise funds for the Statue
of Liberty, whose pedestal the poem has graced since 1903. While
thinking of the statue, the poem was clearly inspired by her lover,
and it's hard today to think of the poem without remembering the
only photograph taken of the two women in 1885, shortly after
Emma had permanently moved into the Dickinson home—those
two literary goddesses standing side by side, staring into the camera, their arms linked together.

Literary critics and generations of doctoral candidates have
done their work on these two women and their relationship, which
as Gertrude Stein wrote in her autobiography, stood out for her
and Alice as a model when they were first crafting the terms of
their own long marriage. I did my own dissertation on the ways in
which the very different women's very different work was shaped
and influenced by the other during their almost twenty years

together. Even in her final years Emily had her own voice and style, which her lover's many contacts brought into book form for the first time. But toward the end of her life, as many have noted, a more formal structure can be found in Dickinson's work, especially in poems like, "Walking in the garden at sunset," and "Standing by window looking out into the yard." We of course see the converse in Emma's work, a lightening up of spirit, more playfulness and experimentation. Her almost singular political thrust was tempered by her relationship, and we can certainly say that Miss Dickinson, who may never have met a living Jew before, took ample opportunity to write about Biblical themes in ways that she hadn't before. I learned her poem on Zion in Hebrew school, as did many others.

It was Lazarus who held the Dickinson family together when Emily's brother Austin abandoned his wife Sue, Emily's beloved friend, and their children, for his lover Mabel Loomis Todd. And although Emily continued to be something of a homebody, the Dickinson household over the years became a haven for the huge Sephardi Lazarus clan, with tempting new smells drifting over the town from the kitchen that had rarely been smelled before in Amherst, to the delight of Emily and Lavinia, who some years later married Emma's cousin Simon da Silva and moved to London with him.

There have been many couples who were both writers. Think of the Brownings, Verlaine and Rimbaud, de Beauvoir and Sartre. But we'd be hard pressed to come up with another couple like Dickinson and Lazarus, from such very different backgrounds, with almost twenty years difference in their ages. And although they were such very different writers both before and after they met, they managed to create a single work—together—that continues to inspire us to this day. We know that between 1894 and 1899 they put together a book of what we today call prose-poems, *Ice Skating on the Moon*. The title comes from a comment made by Emma's great niece Alice after she and her sisters (who called them both Auntie Emzy behind their backs) were told that they were not allowed to go skating at night on the town pond. Alice said, "But Aunties, it would be just like ice skating on the moon!" To which the two women burst out laughing, infuriating the girls, who they promised to make it up to—in another way.

I grew up reading the thirty-six poems they compiled for the girls, and I love the image of the two of them sitting side by side at a table lit by a kerosene lamp, dipping pen in ink and thinking, and pausing, and writing, each a few words, a few lines, in their two very different hands, one so neatly slanted and one a wild scrawl. Can't you picture them, warm shoulders lightly pressed together, getting older and growing more in love, as the end of the very last poem reveals so beautifully, in words that are so fully the marriage of their different styles and voices:

> I turn to you—
> on the moon
> and
> take your hand in mine—
> cold as the night—
> No
> my dear
> warm as your heart—
> which
> never stops beating
> its pulsing words.

Oscar in the Wild West

WHEN WE THINK ABOUT Oscar Wilde and his long amazing life we cannot help but compare him to his most comic character, Philip the Delicate, Duke of Burgundy, who ran away from home in the 16th century and arrived three hundred years later in California, where he met and married Singing Deer, a local Indian chieftain. Of course the two lived happily ever after. Philip, the hero of *Dancing on the Edge of the World,* which premiered in San Francisco on December 20th, 1925, has so shaped American culture, especially American gay culture, that it's hard to believe that in the late 1800s Wilde, worn down from prison and poverty, was at "Death's Door," the imaginary Middle Eastern desert location in which he set the first act of that play. Clearly the play was an inspiration for Virginia Woolf's marvelous *Orlando,* an even more extended romp through history, and was also the inspiration for a Disney children's film made sixty years later, which unsurprisingly left out the love story—What would Oscar think?—but won for itself *an* Oscar.

We know that Wilde fell in love with America on his first visit, a Grand Counter-Tour, not of The Continent, as gentlemen of his time and class were supposed to make, but a wild and wonderful year-long journey that took him from New York to San Francisco in 1882. He was not yet thirty, and while vilified by the press for his outlandish, effeminate garb and attitudes, Wilde became the beloved of miners, cowboys, and factory workers, who recognized in his dilettantism a call to freedom that they could understand.

It was in San Francisco that Wilde did *not* meet the great love of life, Leland Stanford Jr, nor meet his father, the former governor and current head of the Central Pacific Railroad, Leland Stanford Sr. or his mother Jane, whose sense of piety and propriety kept them and their fourteen year old son away from Wilde's talk at Platt's Hall, titled "Art Decoration! Being the Practical Application of the Esthetic Theory to Everyday Home Life and Art Ornamentation!" (Yes, with exclamation points.) The Stanfords did not encounter Wilde while he was staying at the Palace Hotel, then the largest hotel in the world, nor at the Bohemian Club, to which they did belong. But years later, when Wilde and Stanford were living together in California, they would joke about how they *almost* met, how they were fated, were destined to meet.

Wilde left San Francisco in April of 1882, in the wake of a barrage of newspaper and pulpit condemnations of his "Sunflower Aestheticism," and Sunflower was the name that Leland and Oscar called the rambling Moorish villa that they built for themselves an hour south of San Francisco, riding on one of Stanford's trains. There are so many photographs of the couple, there and at their home in the city, always looking so joyous, smiling with a delight that today makes us say of them, with envy—"Now *they* were soul-mates." And yet, much as there was joy in their lives, it was Death that brought them together. By all accounts, when they met in 1897, Wilde, after two difficult years in prison, was weak and ailing. This was something that Leland Stanford Jr. could identify with, as in 1884 he himself had been at Death's Door, having contracted typhoid fever on a trip with his parents to Europe, which nearly killed him. He was weak for years, indulged by his parents, an only child born late in their marriage. Stanford Sr. died in 1893, at which time their son was strong enough to take over the business of running the Central Pacific, and it was five years later that Leland Junior, an amateur archaeologist, finally persuaded his mother to make a return trip to Europe, so that she could look at art and he could purchase artifacts for the growing museum he opened in downtown San Francisco, which was destroyed in the 1906 Big Quake, and rebuilt by Leland in its present home in Golden Gate Park.

It was August of 1897. Three months out of prison, Wilde and Alfred Douglas, the lover who had nearly destroyed his life, were preparing for a reunion. In his first American play, *Vultures in the*

Birdbath, Wilde would write a parody of his own mad foolish attachment to the younger man, but in 1897 he was still obsessed with him, and the two were due to meet that day for the first time since his release, at a little café in Rouen. Wilde, highly anxious, got there early. Sitting on the veranda of the café were Leland and his mother. She was the one who pointed out the bent emaciated man as the once-famous writer. Leland had read his novel, all of his plays, all of his essays, and although he was almost the same age that day as Wilde had been when he made his tour of America, Leland was still a virgin, who knew that he was drawn to older men. But that day, he wasn't thinking romance; he was thinking gratitude, for the many books purchased by indulgent if somewhat critical parents in expensive leather-bound editions, which had made him laugh as could nothing else in the world. In fact, he had practically memorized all of *The Importance of Being Earnest.*

I quote the moment from the memoir Wilde wrote toward the end of his life:

> *I saw coming toward me a handsome young man with a grin on his pale lovely face. He bowed, and in a broad unlikely American accent said, "Mr. Wilde, I believe." I nodded, little knowing then that I was saying yes to the next almost five decades of my life. I extended my hand. He introduced himself. I knew exactly who he was. He said, "My mother and I would be most grateful if you would join us." I replied that I was expecting someone, in about an hour. He said my guest could certainly join us. But long before that guest arrived, the three of us had taken off, escaping my reunion with Douglas, to visit the cathedral that Monet had made so famous in his breathtaking series of paintings, one of which the Stanfords had purchased. It hangs over our bed at Sunflower Ranch.*

When we think of Wilde we tend to forget the years in prison, the breakup of his marriage and the estrangement from his sons Cyril and Vyvyan, which lasted till their mother's death in 1898. We may remember that they later joined Wilde in America, but we almost always forget Lord Alfred Douglas, as increasingly did Wilde himself, so well eclipsed in his heart was he by Leland Stanford.

No, instead we remember the eighteen plays that Oscar wrote in America, the early films that were made of them, several of which he directed himself. After the Bible and Shakespeare, Oscar Wilde is the most quoted writer in the English-speaking world, and all of us have our favorites. And what we remember too is not just Sunflower, the home they built for themselves at Mayfield Grange, the 650 acre property that Stanford Sr. bought near Palo Alto, but also the art colony there that the two of them created, which they named Isola, after Wilde's beloved sister, who died when he was twelve.

In 1911 the two men took a slow train trip back East, for the opening of Wilde's play, *Men Who Knit*. During the three month trip they visited several art colonies including Yaddo and McDowell, and on the train ride back to San Francisco, in a private car with its own kitchen and dining room, Leland suggested to Oscar that they use the land to start a colony of their own, "for people like us." It's hard to imagine gay life in America today without Isola. Late in life, Willa Cather did some of her best writing there, as did Truman Capote, Louise Bogan, Tennessee Williams, May Sarton, and Marilyn Monroe and her lover Billie Holiday, who met in an AA meeting, all of that in the years after both of its founders were dead. We all know the picture of James Dean and Frank O'Hara taken by their good friend Annie Liebovitz, the two of them sprawled out by the pool in lounge chairs, holding hands. Of course O'Hara was for many years the director of Isola, where he wrote his most notable essays and poems, including "You Asked For My What?" which along with poems by Rumi and Mary Oliver are high on the list of inspirational texts given to parents and others to read at lesbian and gay weddings. And the list could go on and on. But in a time when it is still a danger to be gay or lesbian, bi or trans in many countries on this planet, we owe such gratitude to Leland and Oscar as Leland offered to Wilde that day in Rouen.

My favorite picture of the two of them was taken in 1935, on the afternoon of the morning when they'd been awakened by a call from Stockholm informing them that Wilde had been awarded the Nobel Prize in literature. The world was torn by war. It was a terrible time. The phone did not stop ringing all day, with friends and others calling from around the world. People may not know that both men were what Wilde called "tongue addicts," who spoke between them eight languages. In a home with multiple phones and phone lines, and servants answering them in all of those different tongues, the two spent the day in repeated conversations. Late in the afternoon two reporters showed up, having driven down to Sunflower Ranch from San Francisco. The four sat out on the back porch as Wilde answered their many questions, read to them from a work-in-progress, *Walt and Pete*, a theatrical extrapolation of *Leaves of Grass*. And then one of their guests took the picture I love best.

Oscar Wilde, old and thin, at eighty-one a year from his death, his skin dry and wrinkled from years out in the sun, has the fingers of his right hand on Leland's drooping left cheek. Leland Stanford at sixty-seven was still out on his horse every morning, riding the hills behind their house, long retired from the railroad, and still running the colony and the ranch. Neither man is looking at the camera. Both are gazing into each other's eyes, with a look of mingled pride and grief. "How can this be happening? Now? Or ever?" their eyes are imploring each other, after more than thirty years together.

After Wilde's death, Stanford wrote, with the usual mixture of deliberate humor and bad taste that so delighted his lover, in his introduction to Wilde's last essay, "The Imperative for Artists and Artistic Types as Peacemakers!"(Yes, with an exclamation point) that was published after Oscar's death:

> I'm so glad that he didn't live long enough to learn about
> the Nazi atrocities. It would have killed him.

Stanford died seven years later. You can visit their joint mausoleum on the property of Sunflower Ranch, with its naked entwined winged angels rising up toward the sky, and these words engraved upon the portico, chosen by Stanford from Wilde's last play, *A Ridiculous Perfection:*

> If God had given dogs wings,
>
> that was how we two
>
> approached each other,
>
> panting.

Marcel in Love

THE SUN WAS STREAMING through the branches of trees along the edge of the broad terrace, casting long dark flickering shadows upon the stones. At the edge was a flight of stairs that led to a path with a fork in it, one branch leading down to the beach, the other along the cliff toward the city. Below on the sands Marcel Proust watched a family picnicking, a large white sheet spread out, a mother, a picnic basket, three little girls prancing, laughing, the wind carrying the sounds of their delight up to him. The waves were rolling in gently, breaking on the sand. Birds were gliding over the sparkling water, and then in the distance he saw coming toward him a solitary walker, who stopped and waved up at him. Roland. He waved back, and turned to pick up his journal:

> How different. How unexpected, even now, after all these years. How far from the cramped dark quarters of Paris. He, in his crisp white trousers and neat white shirt, is now coming toward me, coming home after his daily constitutional. It is morning here in Algiers, and I am filled with light, sky, and the vast openness of everything around me—and till the day I die I will remember that first night. I was heading off to a party, but the rain was pounding down, relentless, as I stood in the doorway, preparing myself. Suddenly a long dark car came round the corner. I turned toward the lights as it splashed its way toward me, stepping back to get out of the spray. It stopped, a back door flung open, a dark head popped out in the dark wet night and yelled, "Monsieur, no one should be out on the street on a night like this. Please allow me to assist you."

It was the night of May 22, 1919. The Great War was over, and an ailing Marcel Proust had done what he often did in those years. He spent the day inside writing, then dressed to go out to dinner with friends at the Ritz, which had become his second home. Exhausted, pushing himself to continue working on his monumental and ever-expanding novel, he was ill, weak, and should not have been out on that wet night, as Roland Massoud, a physician, recognized, when he had his driver stop the car and call out to the man he'd seen about town, been introduced to before by mutual friends, and whose haunting words he had read, as slowly one then another volume of his long great novel made their way into print.

> *I meant to say—"No thank you, Monsieur Massoud." I was about to. But there was something in his eyes, both kind and imploring. I puzzled over that look as one puzzles over a menu, exploring the various choices. Was his kindness for me? If so, I didn't want it. Such kindness always leaves one feeling uncomfortable, as if something is owed that one may not be well enough to return. But if the kindness was just for him, an aspect of him, then I was insulted, wanting it to be about me. Either way, I realized, I was doomed to stand out in the rain, walk in the rain, continue slogging through it. But something rose up in me, in the space between those large dark eyes and my own sad weary ones, and I said, "Yes."*

Proust remembered meeting Massoud once at the Ritz, sitting with Gide and a few other friends, and another time at a crowded gathering at the home of Cocteau, but it was only at dinner that evening that the two men actually spoke. In speaking they discovered the curious parallels in their lives. Proust, one of two sons of a French father and a Jewish mother, Massoud one of two sons of a Jewish Algerian father and a French mother. Three years younger than Proust—who was still recovering from the heartbreaking death of his last beloved, Alfred Agostinelli, who had always kept him at a distance—Roland had a kind warmth in his eyes. His attention to Marcel reminded him of his younger great love, Reynaldo Hahn, which both attracted him and kept him at a distance. He could almost hear Reynaldo, who had become his most loyal friend over the years, say to him: "Marcel, give him a chance. Don't push him away because you prefer to be pursuing and hate to be pursued."

That dinner led to others. By day Proust sequestered himself with his writing, but gradually he allowed the busy doctor to drop in for lunch once a week, then twice. As spring gave way to summer their intimacy deepened, and as summer gave way to fall Roland slowly began to unravel a scheme that had long seemed vital to him—to get Marcel out of that dark damp apartment and take him to recuperate in the healing warmth of his family's home on the Mediterranean coast outside of Algiers. Heartened by receiving the Légion d'honneur and then by the publication of the first part of *The Guermantes Way*, the third book in his unfolding novel, *In Search of Lost Time*, Marcel Proust agreed to go with Dr. Roland Massoud to Algiers for a month in winter. That month as we know turned into the rest of his life, in fact twenty years longer than his ill-health at the time would have allowed, had he remained in Paris.

> *He is coming up the stairs, smiling and waving again. He turns around, his broad back to me, to watch the laughing sisters turning cartwheels in the sand. I used to sit here in shadow, beneath a large umbrella, afraid of the sun. How long ago that now seems, the sun as much a part of my healing as he himself has been. Then he turns again and waves again, this handsome man who loves me.*

It was on that terrace that Marcel Proust was able to finish and see published each of the eight volumes of *In Search of Lost Time*, just as he wanted it to be, the book received with great acclaim around the world. A rippling gift, Hart Crane and Federico Garcia Lorca met on that terrace, both of them visiting the famous author. And it was there too that they received guests ranging from Virginia Woolf, a new friend, to André Gide, a dear older one of Marcel's. Gide's one great quarrel with Proust about *In Search of Lost Time* was that in heterosexualizing so many of his gay friends, the gay characters who remained never came across as good or kind people. Gide thought that Proust was painting a distorted picture of their tribe, but Proust felt a commitment to the five thousand page novel he had devoted so many years to. Fortunately for us, he took his revenge as he began to plot out the book that we remember as an even greater accomplishment, *Dancing Into the Future,* his final novel and the perfect bookend and companion to the other.

> *He stepped upon the path toward the terrace. In a moment I shall put down this pen so that I can rise and greet him. Lunch will be brought out at any moment. We will sit here together looking out at the sea, and he will ask me how my morning went, and pause to see if I might be in the mood, for I am still moody, to tell him what I have been writing. And if he discerns that I today am open to that question, he will ask it. And in return I will tell him, "I have been writing about you, my darling."*

In Search of Lost Time was a work of mining, of archaeology, of Proust digging deep into his past and into the pasts of all the people he knew, many of them outraged when they read how he had used them in his work, showing them in unflattering (but often true) lights. Some literary critics have said that *In Search of Lost Time* is not actually a novel at all, but a fictionalized autobiography or memoir, the names of historical figures changed, or several merged to create still-identifiable composites. *Leaning Into the Future* is such a very different work, as you must have seen yourself. Although the connection between the main characters, Claude and Ousmane, is clearly based on Roland and himself, it's otherwise almost entirely a work of imagination, set in an imaginary French colony somewhere in Central Africa. Claude is a French physician assigned to a clinic in the closing years of the Great War, the First World War. Ousmane, a native soldier drafted into the French army, finds himself a patient in that clinic, wounded in combat in the closing days of the war. The criticisms Gide had of his earlier book were all met head-on by Proust in this one. He'd never allowed himself before to write about two men falling in love and setting up housekeeping together. But here, in this book, as we know, he did just that.

> It wasn't the morning light, or the clattering of palm fronds outside the window that woke him. It was the

choked cry of Ousmane beside him in his sleep, calling
out from another nightmare.

Proust used what we today would call Ousmane's PTSD to
explore the pernicious effects of cultural homophobia on gay people, deeper than his war wound. And as the war ends and Claude
considers returning to France, and decides not to, but to remain
with his beloved, they begin to confront effects of the racism and
colonization on the lives of the people around them. We know how
the two of them struggle to find a way to work for the liberation
of Claude's adopted and Ousmane's native country. We meet the
friends they make, far from the gardens and drawing rooms of
Proust's earlier work. We see them in native villages, at community
gatherings and dances, two men from different races and from
such very different backgrounds building a shared life together.

Proust died in the midst of the Second World War, in a world
torn apart again, but his last book is one of light and hope. Echoing
his and Roland's ongoing work, which Roland continued after his
death, Ousmane and Claude become engaged in the work of con-
fronting and healing the wounds caused by colonialism, and the
lush interior writing of his earlier work fans out here in ways that
could not have been imagined before, as we find echoed in a small
card that Ousmane penned to his beloved, attached to the birthday
present he'd purchased for him—a wooden carving of two naked
African men embracing—the same statute that Roland had given
to Marcel for one of his birthdays:

> For now, let us rest, my beloved, on your special day. The
> war still rages around us. We cannot do anything to stop
> it. But we can together meet the world that it's happening
> in, day after day after day—with love and kindness. And
> when it's over, dear Claude, for surely it will be—then
> people like us will fan out around the world, bringing
> a message of peace and love and beauty and kindness
> wherever we go. So I reach out to you now, you smelling
> so salty-sweet of your pulsing delicious warm self, and
> I wish you a happy birthday and a year of blessings, the
> two of us hand in hand, together.

From My Raft of a Bed

HOW MANY CHILDREN AROUND the world saw the film *Gigi* when it came out in 1958, and how many of them, chiefly little straight girls and gay boys I imagine, memorized all the songs and still sing them to this day, as I do? And I wonder how it was that their parents had no trouble taking them to see a musical film about a young girl being trained in early 20th century Paris to become a courtesan by her grandmother and great aunt. The film won nine Oscars and I wonder too how many of the parents who took their children to see it—when Colette's name flashed on the silver screen—had ever heard of the author whose novella inspired the film.

Born Sidonie-Gabrielle Colette to a tax collector and his wife in a small town in Burgundy, France, one might say that she used the energy released by the telescoping down of her name into her multiple careers as a writer, mime, actress, and journalist. Her biography reads like a fantasy novel, an erotic thriller, one of those fast-paced beach books that are impossible to put down. First there was Henry Gauthier-Villars, the philandering older first husband she met when she was sixteen, married when she was twenty, and under whose name her first four successful coming-of-age novels were published, not her own. After their divorce she was partnered for a time with novelist Natalie Clifford Barney and then for a number of years with a woman who was also some years her senior, Mathilde de Morny, a marquise, and their on-stage kiss caused a near-riot in the theater. Her second husband, Henry de Jouvenal, was the father of her only child, a daughter named Colette, and while both had had other lovers the marriage ended when her husband discovered that Colette had seduced his sixteen year old son from his first marriage, Bertrand. A year after their divorce Colette married a man fifteen years her junior, Maurice

Goudeket, who she was with for twenty-nine years. He was Jewish, arrested by the Gestapo during the Nazi occupation and then released, thanks to the intervention of a friend—but they spent the remaining war years in a state of terror. That third husband was an adoring fan and a loyal cheerleader as she found herself increasingly confined to her bed, a victim of crippling arthritis, yet still writing, and they both seem to have had discreet affairs with others—a seemingly perfect match.

Colette's world is one of sensuality and physicality, a world of the senses: of sights, sounds, smells, colors, and textures. A stately tree, a glowing lamp, a lush garden, a purring cat, evoked for her readers a spirit far more pagan than anything from her Christian upbringing. Her stories are a multifaceted account of the lives of women: of their marriages, lovers, seductions, and betrayals. She explored poverty, fear, desire, hope, and another great love of hers, not of the flesh but of what preserves flesh—food—in more than fifty novels and several collections of short stories.

There are many doorways into Colette's writing. Let us step through this one—the opening passage to *Break of Day*, which she wrote after the breakup of her second marriage, about the end of love and the return to independent life. In it Colette quotes a letter from her seventy-six-year-old mother to that second husband, declining his invitation to visit her beloved daughter—because her pink cactus was about to blossom, as it did every fourth year. The love between mother and daughter, the palpable vitality of both women and of that rare pink cactus the aged mother did not want to chance missing when it blossomed, and the way that that letter remained an inspiration to Colette long after it was sent—are deeply moving, highly inspirational. But in truth, Colette neglected her mother just as she did her only child, also named Colette but usually called Bel-Gazou—her own father's nickname for her—who was raised by nurses and rarely saw her famous mother. And that lovely letter and others from her mother found in her books were seriously edited to reflect well upon herself.

We may feel sorry for the young woman taken in by that first husband, who forced her to crank out books published in his own name, even as we celebrate his getting her started as a writer, but keeping the rights to her writing after she left him, which launched her onto the stage in order to support herself. But in her relationship with the marquise and her next two husbands we find ourselves asking—"Was there love there, or love as we want to know it—mutuality?" In a sense, yes. The mutuality of Colette-the-lover came from this—"We are both in love with me. How lovely!" So she basked in the adoration of her third husband, sharing a wonderful apartment in the Palais-Royal, looking out at its wonderful gardens, where Colette the grande dame received visitors in her magnificent throne of a bed. Truman Capote described her as, "Reddish, frizzy" with "rather African-looking hair, slanting, alley-cat eyes rimmed with kohl . . . rouged cheeks . . . lips thin and tense as wire but painted a really brazen hussy scarlet."

In 1954 Japanese artist Fumi Yamada was visiting Paris. Great-niece of the ukiyo-e painter Hiroshige, she was there in her capacity as a master of the art of Sumi-e ink-brush painting and also of Ikebana, flower arranging. In those postwar years when Japan was still often viewed as an enemy power, Yamada was part of a group of seven artists traveling the world as cultural ambassadors. They had just been in New York, lecturing at the Museum of Modern Art, then London where Yamada had lived with her diplomat husband in the early years of their marriage. Paris was the last stop on the way home. Her husband had been part of the Japanese delegation to Paris Peace Conference at the end of World War One. They remained in Paris for the creation of the League of Nations and it was then that Colette and Fumi first met through mutual friends. In fact the two couples dined together several times, but the two women had not seen each other since 1933 when Japan left the League and Yamada and her husband returned to Tokyo.

Picture a distinguished woman in her seventy-seventh year, still mourning the loss of her husband, who had died in the bombing of Nagasaki. Grey hair pulled back in a tight bun, wearing a dark elegant suit from Christian Dior, her heels clicking on the parquet floor, she approaches that large bed and its noted resident. Yamada described what happened next in Japanese quickly written to the side of a brush painting of Colette she did that evening, back in her hotel:

> *Struck*
>
> *Face alien and familiar*
>
> *Looming up from quilted bed*
>
> *Scented hand extended*
>
> *Changes everything*

A few years ago I bought a used copy of Colette's last wonderful book, *From My Raft of a Bed*, at The Strand Book Store in Manhattan, and found this passage underlined in red ink:

> How could a face so alien, or her rusty French, cut through me as nothing else, as no one else ever had? How could she become, not just the perfect mirror in whose dark eyes I saw my true self, but a mirror that revealed to me how armored like a medieval soldier I had been in the arms of every lover since the first? I began to tremble as her painter's gaze took me in, and I knew in that moment that I had finally met my equal. She asked if I was cold. I invited her to sit down. My husband left the room. Left me alone with her. Grown so old, my defenses so blessedly weak from age and pain, all I could do was invite her to bring her chair closer, which she did, sliding it over the polished parquet floor. Then we each reached out a hand. And so it was, at age eighty, that my life, my true life, began.

Startling, unexpected. One woman of eighty years, the other seventy-seven. Painter looking at writer. Writer looking back. This is what multilingual Yamada wrote in English above a brush painting of Colette leaning close to kiss her for the first time:

> *Not fall, I told my analyst*
>
> *on the phone*
>
> *of hunger so long denied*
>
> *no, we rose*
>
> *two old women*
>
> *one crippled, one bent*

we rose in love

two creaking fledglings

elegant again

Elegantly, Yamada returned to Tokyo, began work on her next book, *Concise, Exquisite,* a collection of ink-brush paintings of Colette's room and bed and wandering cats. Elegantly, Colette's third husband soon moved in with the mistress he would later marry, and then Yamada returned to Paris, where she lived with her beloved for the last three years of her life. Delightfully, the two couples often socialized together, seated around that raft of a bed. Her neighbor and old friend Jean Cocteau noted the change that came over Colette: "Not her incessant observation, brilliant and wearying, but at long last—true connection." It was Yamada who encouraged her to reach out to Bel-Gazou and overcome her (ironic) disdain for her daughter being a lesbian, and in her last years they grew close in a new way, as Bel-Gazou noted herself: "She who handed me a cup of tea, that gnarled hand that wrote so much, did it, for the first time, smiling tenderly."

In her final book, a series of letters to her great love, Colette wrote:

> Thank you for that swift moment in which you, with your gardener's shears, snipped away the stony cowl that had covered me since birth.

In her poem, "Bonsai lover," Colette describes herself as a root-bound creature who finally burst forth in red flowers, like her mother's pink cactus. And in her final interview, given six months before she died in 1958, Colette said:

> If I could trade these last three years for all that went before, I would, if I weren't so sure that those eighty years prepared me for them.

So we picture the two, seated in a room that looked out on a vast public garden, one of them in her bed and the other at her painting desk, or preparing a cup of tea, the two of them writing and painting in tandem, looking up, laughing, at private jokes.

Later, one curling up with the other, rubbing her aching limbs with herb-scented oils, kissing her temples, singing her Japanese lullabies. That other, running her fingers through the other's long gray undone hair, asking, "Darling, how is the painting going?" Telling her, "This tea is delicious." Asking, "What are you thinking of doing next?" Purring in her ear like one of their four cats.

Due to her three divorces, when Colette died the Catholic Church refused to give her a religious burial. But in a picture taken at her state funeral we see beside her casket the two surviving ex-husbands and all of their children including Bel-Gazou and her partner Rebka Melaku, standing beside Bertrand, the stepson Colette seduced all those years before. They're all clustered around Fumi Yamada, who is holding a copy of *From My Raft of a Bed* and her own just-published book of brush paintings of her lover, *Delicious Plum,* both of which she placed in the open casket.

Yamada returned to Tokyo after Colette's death and spent the last five years of her life translating her lover's work into Japanese, as well as publishing two more books of her own sumi-e paintings. At her death her ashes were interred in Colette's grave at Père-Lachaise Cemetery, with its large dark stone that looks to many like the headboard of an enormous bed. Below the inscription of Colette's name and dates are carved in Roman letters and Japanese characters Fumi Yamada's name and dates, and below them, in French and Japanese, are these words from *From My Raft of a Bed:*

Only two wizened hands
can hold eternity.

A Woolf in Zabar's

PRONE TO BOUTS OF madness throughout her life, fearing that they were returning and that this time she would not be able to fight them off, on March 28, 1941, Virginia Woolf left a brief good-bye note for her sister Vanessa, another one for her husband Leonard, slipped out their country home, Monk's House, and headed through the garden and across a field toward the River Ouse, with the intention of drowning herself. She'd recently finished a solid draft of a new novel, *Between the Acts,* which Leonard had praised; but she'd lost faith in it, and the voices she'd been hearing on and off for years had returned, fueled by the nightmares of the war and the bombing and destruction in London, which had forced them to leave the city. But, this was something she'd thought about for years, and walking slowly along the banks of the river she began to gather large stones, dropping them into the capacious pockets of her heavy winter coat.

Exhausted after three months without a single day off, on March 28, 1941, American Army nurse Doris Lefkowitz, stationed nearby, left the barracks she was living in and headed off to explore the land around the River Ouse, which she had read about in a regional guide she'd borrowed from one of the surgeons. It was a lovely morning, clear and blustery, with the very faintest hints of spring in the air; the kind of weather she liked: bracing, wild around the edges. In her pocket Lefkowitz had a small herring sandwich, wrapped in wax paper, and a small thermos of coffee tucked into the purse which hung from a long strap over her shoulder. She was exhausted physically and emotionally, as the war dragged on, as the constant bombing of England continued. She was worn out from the agony, the hopelessness, the wounds, the mangled bodies, the blood, the screaming, the constant death.

As she came around a bend in the road she saw a lone figure up ahead, wearing a dark overcoat, her head wrapped in a dark kerchief. She was walking along at a brisk yet odd pace, seeming to be both pushed ahead and yet held back at the same time. As she got closer Lefkowitz could sense the thrust of the mission she was on, and, watching the way her long winter coat hung, its pockets bulging—she understood.

Not wanting to startle her, she was startled herself when the woman turned to her for a moment, a wild desperate look in her eyes, then quickly looked away, and continued on. But in that turning Lefkowitz recognized her. She'd read many of her books, was deeply influenced by *A Room of One's Own* when she read it at Brooklyn College, and knew something of the story of her romantic friendship with Vita Sackville-West, which had helped her in her own struggles with her slowly blossoming sexuality. She'd even heard Woolf speak a few years earlier on the radio, that elegant patrician voice coming out of the large wooden cabinet. She knew too a bit about her life, her mental instability, and as a nurse, even an exhausted nurse on her one day off in months, Doris Lefkowitz's brain was racing, desperate as Woolf began to move out of range. Suddenly, remembering the rich wonderful voice she'd heard before, she found herself calling out, "Excuse me, Madame. Excuse me," in a raw Brooklyn voice that seemed to jar the very air around them and shake the very few newly forming buds on the surrounding trees.

Woolf stopped in her tracks, her patrician face trembling. Lefkowitz watched as with monumental will Woolf rearranged herself, and said, in the rich resonant tones that lived behind all of her extraordinary writings: "Yes, dear. Can I help you?"

Moving slowly, Doris Lefkowitz walked closer. "Thank you so much," she said, pausing a few feet away. "I seem to have gotten myself lost." Woolf sighed, and with a forced smile said something neither of them could remember later. Lefkowitz came closer and said, "I am so lost, and so desperately cold," although she was neither, and Woolf responded just as she hoped she would. She informed the young woman that she lived nearby and invited her home for a cup of tea, which Lefkowitz accepted, ignoring the coffee in her purse as she ignored the stones in Woolf's pockets. And in that moment, the smile that Lefkowitz gave Virginia seemed to fill her soul, to feed her, in a way that she had not felt in years. She did not know yet that Lefkowitz, who soon introduced herself, and was wearing her one civilian outfit, was a nurse. She did not know that that nurse had noted the stones dragging her down, and she did not know yet that that younger woman with the strange accent she could only identify as New York, would soon slip an arm through her own as they turned to walk back to the house.

Years later Woolf wrote about that day, how Doris began to chat about the trees, about how much she loved England, about her hope that the war was coming to an end, in a manner that was both comforting and curiously engaging to someone intent on taking her life just moments before. And when, moments later, a long-faced man in a straw hat came racing toward them, his coattails flapping behind him, Woolf had forgotten about the suicide notes she'd left behind, Doris had recognized the husband, and did what she'd done before. She called out, "Oh, hello. You must be Mr. Woolf. I'm Doris Lefkowitz. And your wife and I are having such a delightful chat."

Leonard himself wrote some years later how different that day might have gone—if Doris Lefkowitz had not appeared out of the blue—if she had not been a trained healer—if Virginia had not been so well-brought up—and lastly, if Doris had not been Jewish, and therefore already family. Looking at the two of them, wife and stranger arm in arm, he knew that something significant had happened. Relieved beyond belief, but startled beyond imagining, utterly trusting the strange American Jewess, he said nothing about the note, or his terror, as the three of them headed back to the house, where Virginia shrugged herself out of her coat and stuffed it in a corner behind an armchair, while their guest looked around with curiosity, as Leonard put up a kettle for the tea they made from plants that grew in their garden. Then the three sat down at the table and continued to chat about this and that, Leonard never taking his eyes off Virginia, and she always looking away.

But Leonard could see his wife relaxing, and he watched the way she looked at the rather lovely red-haired stranger with the great relief that only a man such as he, who had gone through so much already with Virginia, could ever have allowed himself to feel.

"You look rather tired," Doris said to her hostess, who suddenly realized that she was. "Why don't you lie down for a bit," Leonard added, to which a weary Virginia replied, "Yes, I think that I shall." She thanked their guest, invited her to come back, and went off to her bedroom, leaving Leonard and Doris to fill each other in on what had happened, each as horrified and relieved as the other. The notes, which he showed her, the stones in her pockets, which they'd all ignored, the darting look in Virginia's eyes, which seemed to slow and almost fade as they sat there talking, all persuaded Leonard to say to Doris, "My wife seems to trust you, instinctively. This has happened to her a few times before, and it's always meant a great deal to me. So I do hope that you will return again, as often as you like." Doris assured him that she would, as often as she could, given her work. In the weeks and months that followed, Virginia, resting under the care of her old physician friend Octavia Wilberforce, slowly returned to health, and even went back to work on what became the final marvelous draft of *Between the Acts*.

In all of history there has been perhaps no more curious a courtship than that of Doris Lefkowitz and Virginia Woolf, entirely conducted under the watchful loving eyes of a cautious and grateful husband. He'd seen the agony that his wife went through during her fiery relationship with Sackville-West, and knew that it had been doomed as much by Virginia's fragile emotional state as it was by her lover's monumental ego. But Doris was different, caring and warm, passionate in a grounded way he recognized from the women in his own family, and it was he who sat Doris down about a year after they met, as the war was still raging, and said, "All I want for Virginia is to be happy, and you can give her a kind of happiness that I am not capable of."

For years Leonard and his second wife Lydia would vacation with Virginia and Doris, who moved to New York after the war was over. Some years they all met up on Cape Cod, where Virginia and Doris bought a small cottage on Truro Beach, and other years they rendezvoused back at Monk's House, where they'd had tea together that first afternoon. Virginia and Doris found a large apartment on the Upper West Side, in a building much populated by Europeans in exile. While Virginia wrote and explored the city, Doris went on to medical school and then worked for many years as a pediatrician. And yes, there were times when Virginia struggled with depression and flickers of madness, but post-war New York was a city of art and jazz and psychotherapists, many who'd fled from Nazi Europe, and all of that, grounded in her relationship with Doris, kept Virginia on an even keel. Plus Doris, through her cousin Milton, who taught at Columbia, landed Virginia a part-time job there, where she was able to teach and lecture as she desired, in fact till the year she died.

I remember my mother telling me that she'd heard Woolf speak at the 92nd Street Y. She said that Woolf was the most open and compassionate human being she had ever encountered. And I think about those iconic photographs of her—the amazing London ones taken by Man Ray in the 1930s, and the Manhattan studio portraits of her taken by Richard Avedon in the 1950s, so elegant in her mid-seventies. But my favorite is the one that Diane Arbus snapped of her in 1961, standing in the courtyard of the Museum of Modern Art, on a windy day, holding her big floppy hat to her head. She was seventy-nine, her magnificent face lined and utterly exquisite, looking into the camera with sheer almost childlike delight. At that age she was still teaching and still writing. In fact she was yet to start, even conceive of, her last and most famous novel. So let's call to mind the highlights of her canon—*Mrs. Dalloway, To the Lighthouse, The Waves, Between the Acts, A City in Spring, The Gilman Sisters, In a Garden of Pleasure,* and her last great masterpiece, *Quite Simply,* that delicious prose-poem tribute to Doris—along with all of the books of essays, the book of Truro poems about their extensive garden—*Seaworthy,* the collected letters, the five volumes of short stories, the seven illustrated children's books, all written for one or another of Doris's nieces and nephews.

We know how cruel the earlier Woolf had been to Leonard, once telling her sister at dinner to "Feed the Jew." But in New York, with Lefkowitz, she changed, mellowed. After all, the iconic photos of her were all taken by Jews, Arbus becoming a close friend over the years, Woolf her confidant and counsel when she herself was contemplating suicide. And how can we not mention Woolf's one astonishing literary collaboration—*A Tale of Two Voices,* the Dickensian novella about Manhattan that she wrote with her good friend and downstairs neighbor Isaac Bashevis Singer.

There are all those interviews with her! I love to watch them on YouTube, talking about art, politics, history, music—articulate, engaging, and funny in constantly unexpected ways, telling Jewish jokes with her British-Yiddish accent: "There was a man from Minsk who traveled to Pinsk . . ." I also like to watch the interview Doris did with Barbara Walters, three years after Woolf died, when her collected essays were being released. Through Lefkowitz's kind hazel eyes we can picture Virginia in Zabar's, the Upper West Side's famous self-described "gourmet epicurean emporium" on a Sunday morning, the *New York Times* under her arm, buying bagels and lox for their breakfast. We can spy on the two of them taking Esperanto classes at the New School, bent over the same faded second-hand textbook. Esperanto, the international language created by L. L. Zamenhof, the Polish Jewish pacifist, peering out into a better (if still unattained) future. And think about Woolf's amazing circle of friends on several continents, and remember the annual seminars she led at Isola, the art colony founded by Oscar and Leland in California, which influenced several generations of queer writers.

Looking back at the culture of Great Books and the contributions of centuries of Dead White Men—I know that everyone singles out one book by George Elliot as our greatest literary work, but I find it heartening to know that when we look at the total oeuvre of Western writers, all critics agree that at the summit is Virginia Woolf, a female Moses, standing in her study, pen in hand—for she always wrote standing up, like an artist at her easel—looking out over Broadway to the Hudson River, sitting on the desk beside her an old yahrzeit glass of black unsweetened tea and a blue and white flower-painted plate of Doris's homemade poppy seed ruglach.

Border Crossing

FRIENDS HAD PRESSURED FRANZ for years. He loved Yiddish theatre, had taken Hebrew classes, but angered his father by his excessive, if cultural, attachment to his Jewishness. And clearly he identified with the Zionist movement, or with some elements of it. But . . . but. There was always a but. His family, his job, his writing. Still, the Great War was over, it was easier to travel, and so many others were going. Palestine seemed their hope. And he was getting older, hadn't been well. But then he recovered, and something shifted in him, so he went, this man who had written in his journal, "What do I have in common with the Jews? I have hardly anything in common with myself." Pale, nervous, pressed in among shipmates he had largely avoided, Franz Kafka stepped off the boat in Haifa carrying a single brown valise in one hand and a German translation of *Walden* in the other.

It was October of 1920. It was hot, it was noisy, it was very different from what he had imagined. The smell in the air—was totally unfamiliar, and as he followed the others in front of him down the gangplank, he remembered a story his grandfather had told him. Was it about Rebbe Nachman? Who longed to go to the holy land, went, got off the ship, felt his feet on the ground, then walked back up the gangplank to go back home. He wanted to go home himself. This place that was supposed to feel like home—looked and smelled and sounded—like another planet. He imagined trees, imagined, he realized, a Walden Pond of his own Eastern European dreaming.

There was chaos ahead. He stopped, put the book in his valise and checked again in his jacket pocket, as he had every few moments, for the name and address of the hostel that a Zionist friend had given him, a Zionist friend who had forgiven him the story

"Jackals and Arabs," that seemed critical of the movement—when he told him he was actually going. And why not? He was alone, again. Why not be alone in a foreign land?

The hostel was crowded, dirty, and noisy. A few days later, from a German-speaking Jewish widow who owned a small produce market, he learned about a small pension on the edge of town, and took his few belongings there. It was owned by a Christian couple, the Hostetlers, who were German-speaking Swiss Mennonites, and Kafka found himself enjoying their company. It was the husband, Johannes, who took him on long walks around the city, for picnics in the hills, and led him to the garden shrine of the Baha'i faith, where their founder, the Bab, was buried. The great shrine we know today hadn't been built yet, but the garden was lovely and Kafka found himself drawn there again and again, frequently writing in his journal and scribbling off postcards to friends and family, describing his adventures. His limited adventures. Friends of friends who'd heard he was there wanted to take him—everywhere. Tel Aviv, Jerusalem, to this or that kibbutz. But all he wanted to do was stay put, stay and explore the place that he was in.

In November of 1920 the Hostetlers invited Kafka to a poetry reading at the home of a Christian Arab family they had met, the Botroses, and Kafka joined them. How like the man we know, the Jew with so little in common with even himself, who found himself avoiding other Jews, particularly those who spoke German, but kept up with his Hebrew lessons—not from a European but from a recent immigrant from Yemen, Mosheh Halevi, in exchange for German lessons, every Tuesday afternoon. And it was in this period that he wrote his first story in Palestine, about the son of the ancient wonder-working rabbi Honi, who could make rain—but whose son Noni could not, and was taunted by others, including his own father, who caused a thunderstorm to brew above his head.

The Botros family were prominent in the city, and the doors of their home were open to everyone, Christians, Muslims, Jews, and Bahá'ís, all of whose faiths the head of the family, Pierre, saw as branches on the same tree. A few weeks before, a Hindu follower of

Mahatma Gandhi had been their guest. Upon hearing about him, Kafka was saddened to have missed him, on his way to London for a conference. A lengthy entry written that night in his journal links the struggle for independence in India with what was going on in Palestine. He wrote less about the poetry reading, other than to say that it was disappointing, "Pompous characters reading about peace with Victorian diction." Nor did he mention the hosts' son Adam, who he also met that night, a tall shy handsome man his own age who worked in the family's textile business. But Adam wrote at length about Kafka in his journal, about his deep penetrating eyes and their short unpenetrating conversation, about being both of them office workers. Adam Botros had read a few of Kafka's stories, and if the conversation had continued he might have told Kafka that he was a poet of sorts, but his sister Maryam interrupted them to offer their guest some more tea, and Adam could sense that their guest was one of those men who are more comfortable in conversation with women, so he slipped away.

Kafka did write about their next meeting, at a large joyous Christmas dinner he and the Hostetlers were invited to by Mr. Botros. After dinner he found himself in the drawing room seated next to his hosts' son, who struck up a conversation with him about Flaubert, who they both enjoyed reading, and about Tolstoy's last book, which they both found disappointing. He also mentioned Adam Botros' startling hazel eyes:

> An inheritance from Crusader ancestors who stayed behind, he told me.

And then there is no mention of him again for two months. But Adam mentioned him, the ways in which Kafka had put up a wall against him, shunning him when they met, no longer responding even to his family's invitations to come visit. With insight Adam wrote:

> This is the sort of man, and I've met him before, who is so afraid of his yearning that he runs from woman to woman like a hungry dog from person to person at the dinner table, begging with big wide desperate eyes that say, "I am

> *starving! No one has fed me in days", until he finds the one*
> *gullible person who will take something off their plate.*

Kafka wrote in his journal in early January of 1923 that he
was ready to go home, as his family was begging him to do. On
January 13th he was crossing the street to the post office when he
was struck down by a passing wagon carrying crates of squawking
chickens. The injury wasn't serious but he did end up in the hospital for three days. Adam had heard initially that he'd been killed,
then later that he'd been seriously injured, and desperate, unafraid,
already in love, he took action and headed to the hospital, bearing
a small potted plant that his grandmother had given him, that sat
on the table beside his bed, a small pot of rosemary, and also a
small edition of *Leaves of Grass* in German, which he dropped in
his jacket pocket, imagining that he might read from it later to the
recovering patient. But he never got around to it—that day.

We know from Kafka's journal entry, written that evening
when he was alone again, what happened:

> *He walked in, looking down at the floor, following a tiny*
> *shriveled nurse in starched white. Then he looked up at me.*
> *He was smiling and extended a small potted plant to me.*
> *I took it. Could smell it. Our fingers touched briefly. And*
> *then it happened. Something broke in me. Broke open. The*
> *horrifying thing I'd scurried around for so many years,*
> *and written about in oblique ways, in stories and in my*
> *journal. The thing that Felice in a moment of anger had*
> *once accused me of. I looked up at him, and a vast seeing-*
> *eye in my heart took him in, in the way a blind person*
> *after a prophet's miracle must take in the first light they are*
> *able to see, squinting and ecstatic at the same time. "This*
> *is it!" I cried out, inside, trembling, as I invited him to sit*
> *in the chair beside my bed. He did, spreading his coattails*
> *out behind him. And then, the sheer white curtains on the*
> *slightly open window behind him blew over him for a mo-*
> *ment, like a bridal veil. Or, was I the bride, new to these*
> *feelings? He smiled again. I knew that I would find out.*

Their relationship grew slowly, each afraid, with so many
differences between them, and so many differences between them

and the many people around them, marrying and having children, people of so many different faiths, and no faith. Over lunch, tea, on longer and longer walks, as Kafka in the heat regained his strength and health, the two grew closer and closer, without a clear word being said. Yet. A short trip to Istanbul, a shared hotel room, that both men wrote about later, marked the beginning of the next step in their union. It was there that Kafka wrote one of his most famous stories, "White Feathers," about a man who is smothered to death by a collapsing wooden cart covered with towering piles of crated chickens. That poor old man dies and instantly comes back—as a rooster who falls in love with another rooster. And it was there that Botros wrote one of his most famous poems, "In the Temple Courtyard," which is often compared to something by Cavafy, about a son of the high priest Caiaphas who is climbing the outer stairs to the great temple in Jerusalem when he sees and instantly falls in love with a Roman centurion, who in un-Cavafy fashion—falls in love with him—and stays in love with him.

Yes, from these quiet beginnings, a great romance was born. Nothing surprising in that. What surprises, however, is what happened next. Friends of Kafka's in Prague were either puzzled or delighted by the joyful, comic stories he wrote in Palestine, but none could have predicted the next chapter in the life of this curious man. In the spring of 1925 Kafka wrote a very short story called "Frau Jacobs' Mirror," about a widow who moves to Palestine after her husband's death, and mysteriously finds in her purse one day a small compact with a mirror inside that is gold and not silver, and which reflects not her own face but someone else's, every time she looks into it. We've all read the story. We know what happens next. Frau Jacobs is walking in the market one day when she sees across a vegetable cart a tall slim Arab woman her own age—the very woman whose face keeps appearing in her little mirror. Shocked at first, then delighted, she follows the woman around the city for weeks until she finally has the courage to approach her in the market. With no shared language between them, Frau Jacobs finds a way to communicate with the other woman, shows her the mirror, in which, lo and behold—her very own Jewish face appears when the Muslim woman looks into it.

That's the whole of Kafka's original story, as you may know. And you probably know the story about the story, how Adam Botros published it in *Levantine Muse*, the small literary journal he created, which featured the works of the local writers who'd read in his parents' parlor, as Kafka had read this one. Kafka mailed a copy to his friend Max Brod in Prague, who sent it to a cousin in Munich, who mailed it to a friend in Johannesburg who sent it on to Hermann Kallenbach in India. Kallenbach read the story to his friend and lover Mohandas Gandhi, in whose hands Kafka's golden mirror of reflecting-others became the perfect metaphor for what he was trying to teach.

When we think about this story, many of us forget that it was Gandhi who invited the final version of the tale of the two women, Fatima and Fanya, who become the best of friends. They aren't named in Kafka's original story, but in the first letter Gandhi wrote to Kafka in November of 1927 he asked if he would continue the tale, to which Kafka wrote back with a new final section, in which he gave the two women the names we know them by. It was Gandhi in his next letter who suggested that Kafka begin to work toward the creation of a unified Palestine—and it's from that time that we can date the shift in Botros's journal, from a purely artistic endeavor to a periodical that expressed the aesthetic and political voices of writers and thinkers from all the varied groups in Palestine—Arab and Jewish, Christian and Muslim, Druze, Baha'i, native born and immigrants—all of them committed to the cause of peaceful cooperation.

Gandhi told that story over and over again, sometimes about two women and sometimes about two men, one Muslim and one Hindu. And Kafka and Botros, partners in life and in work, told the story of the golden mirror at meetings and rallies, at demonstrations and marches, in the context of their own at-times volatile community. As the situation in Europe worsened, Kafka and Botros sent for Kafka's parents, sisters, and their families, who settled in different cities and kibbutzim in Palestine. Kafka's youngest and favorite sister, Ottla, divorced in Europe, remarried an older widowed Muslim friend of the Botros clan, lawyer Mufid Halabi, and they worked together after the war to integrate European Jews arriving in Palestine into local culture and communities.

The years after the war were not easy, with repeated outbursts of violence and hostility between Arabs and Jews. But Kafka's story, that little story, was told and retold, in Yiddish and Arabic, Hebrew and Turkish and a host of other languages, to natives and immigrants, to the elderly and to children in every school in every village and city, until it became as much a part of the culture as the timeless rocky hills, the remains of ancient history, the Mediterranean beaches, the olive groves, the smell of fresh baked pita, and the wonderful blend of music and dancing from around the world.

Hanging over my desk as I type is a framed photograph of Adam and Franz, arms linked, telling that story in 1948 from a theatre stage in Haifa. I've sat in that theatre several times over the years, listening to a recording of the two men, in their matching jackets and ties, reading alternate paragraphs of the story in Hebrew and Arabic. Perhaps you've sat there too, in that elegant art deco theatre, listening to them read and then listening to the voices of Mufid Halabi its first prime minister, and Martin Buber its first president, as they declare Haifa to be the capital of the newly independent bi-national Federation of Palestine.

Can we say that a simple five-page story could shape history? That would be naïve. So many factors shift and change through time. But sometimes a story has the power to become a collective dream, as did this one. And as Adam Botros wrote in his tribute to his life partner, *The Muses' Muse,* published three years after Kafka's death in 1964:

> Had I a crystal ball, or a different kind of mirror, I might gaze into it and see a very different course of history unfolding. It isn't hard to imagine that when the British granted independence to India and Palestine, that those new nations might have erupted into bloodshed, war, and fragmentation. Instead, because of one little story and its charming coda, India is one free nation, home

to Hindus, Muslims, Jains, Sikhs and others, all of them living in peace—and Palestine is one free nation, home to Jews, Muslims, Christians, Druze, Baha'i's and others, all of us living together in peace. For, as my dear Franz used to say, "Writing is prayer." And in our day and age, the greatest saints and prophets are storytellers, and the greatest prayer of all is the prayer for peace, answered in our time.

The End

The decisive moment in human evolution is perpetual.

FRANZ KAFKA, *APHORISMS*

It might as well be this that
rakes the new moons away

JOSEPH MCKAY, "AT LAMMAS"

Pass me a rearrange.
the sun the same taste.

GERARD RIZZA, "REGARD FOR JUNCTION"

. . . an old, established and famous composer assembling the
man's correspondence and musical manuscripts for dona-
tion to a large library.

CHRISTOPHER COX, "NEUROTIC MOON"

Eleven is a number of teaching, of seers, and faith,
of patience, honesty, and spiritual illumination,
a master number because of the way that it repeats,
likewise it is the number of the light within all selves,
and it draws some special few to the vast unknown.

LYNNE REYNOLDS, "ON SQUIRREL HILL"

Tinkerings

BELOW ARE THE NAMES and dates of the historical characters in this book. The smaller middle ones are the dates of their actual death; the last dates are when they died in the parallel reality that's my invented truth.

Jane Austen	1775	*1817*	1856
Henry David Thoreau	1817	*1862*	1887
George Eliot	1819	*1880*	1893
Leo Tolstoy	1828	*1910*	1913
Emily Dickinson	1830	*1886*	1902
Emma Lazarus	1849	*1887*	1914
Oscar Wilde	1854	*1900*	1936
Leland Stanford Jr.	1868	*1884*	1943
Marcel Proust	1871	*1922*	1942
Colette	1873	*1954*	1958
Virginia Woolf	1882	*1941*	1963
Franz Kafka	1883	*1924*	1964

This book emerged from a dream in which Jane Austen fell in love with an American sea captain, but in the story I ended up writing, years later, she fell in love with his daughter. The one historical non-writer in the book is Leland Stanford Jr., who died of typhus when he was fifteen. For eight years I lived up the block, around the corner, and across the street from the school his devastated parents founded in his memory. Its official name is Leland Stanford Junior University, and I often went walking there, in the lovely arboretum where he and his parents are buried.

It never occurred to me to write about Walt Whitman, but I mulled over stories about Hart Crane, saved from suicide, and Federico Garcia Lorca, saved from being murdered—by the men they spent the rest of their long happy lives with. I thought about giving James Baldwin a much longer life, in which he fell in love with a version of me. I could have written about May Sarton, who I met once and exchanged letters with for several years. And what could I have done with the lives of June Jordan and Audre Lorde, both of whom I knew and wish had lived for so much longer?

I also imagined stories about my lovers Joseph McKay, who like a magnet attracted the adventures that he spun into poems and bedtime stories, and Gerard Rizza, whose first and only book of poems, *Regard for Junction,* came out shortly after he died—and about my first editor Chris Cox, a wonderful published writer and member of the noted gay men's writing group The Violet Quill. But every attempt I made to write about them brought me pain—because they all died of AIDS. Much too young! But if this book ever has an extended life of its own (which is entirely up to the muses)—it will include them, the authors I mentioned above, my sister-friend Lynne Reynolds, an amazing artist, writer, and architect who died as this book was moving toward publication—and Goddess knows who else.

Author Bio
Fictional

ANDREW OMAR RAMER WAS born in Paris on March 24, 1951. When he was five his British diplomat father and Persian journalist mother moved to Tokyo, where his sister Lynne was born, and when he was ten the family moved to Washington DC. In sixth grade his teacher Jerome Winetsky read the class Robert Frost's poem, "The Road Not Taken" which begins: "Two roads diverged . . . ." Shaken to the core, Ramer went home, wrote his first poem, and never stopped writing.

Ramer studied English literature at Harvard, but his sister Lynne encouraged him to abandon his dissertation (on lesbian subtexts in the novels of the Brontë sisters) and devote himself to his own writing. In 1976 he moved to Seattle to be with a man he met at a writing conference, who soon dumped him. But he stayed there, got a job in a used bookstore, and finished, illustrated, and sold his first book, *little pictures*, which he began writing in college. The book was edited by Chris Cox and published in 1977. His second book came out in 1980, *Twenty-two Views of a Life,* an autobiography told through objects, also edited by Cox. Later that year Ramer moved in with Argentinean poet Raul Meller, who he met under the trees at an outdoor Shabbat service, and the following year he wrote in his journal: "A new disease has stormed in—like a fire-barfing dragon."

Raul was diagnosed with AIDS in 1983 and died in 1984. When the HIV test was approved in 1985 Ramer took it, knowing what the results would be. It was then that he completed his next book, *Four Roads Diverged,* in which he explored the ways that English and American literature would have been different if Charles Dickens and Mark Twain had died as young men, and how

Jewish storytelling would have been different if Sholem Aleichem and I. L. Peretz had also died young.

Forever After was Ramer's next book, a queer retelling of the lives of twenty of his favorite writers, starting with the Biblical prophetess Huldah, Sappho, and the medieval Spanish rabbi Yehudah Halevi, who wrote love poems to young men that Ramer was never taught about in Hebrew School. They're followed by stories about Sufi poet Jalaluddin Rumi, philosopher Baruch Spinoza, haiku writer Matsuo Basho, and of course the Brontë sisters—Charlotte, Emily, and Anne—along with stories about George Sand, Nikolai Gogol, Walt Whitman, D. H. Lawrence, Zora Neale Hurston, Djuna Barnes, Dorothy Parker, Langston Hughes, Clarice Lispector, Yukio Mishima, and his beloved partner Raul.

Nine months after *Forever After* was published, following the path of writers including Anna Akhmatova and Fyodor Dostoevsky (who was not one of his favorites) Ramer took all of his unpublished work—typed stories, novels, essays, poems, and the forty-seven composition notebooks in which he'd been keeping his handwritten journal—out to the patio behind his Queen Anne Hill home, where he and Lynne burned them in the barbecue pit that he and Raul built when they bought the house. Ramer died of AIDS ten days later, on September 15, 1987, the one hundredth anniversary of Thoreau's death.

Author Bio
Factional

ANDREW RAMER WAS BORN on March 24, 1951 in Elm/hurst, Queens, New York, across the street from an amusement park called Fairyland, and since 2016 he's lived in Oak/land, California, up the street from an amusement park called Fairyland. (The slash marks in those locations are deliberate. Ramer is a great lover of trees and the books that come from them.) His brother Richard was born in 1953, in a different hospital, and in 1956 the Ramers moved to Long Island. Four years later their father left home, putting an end to any "happily ever after" for that small suburban family.

It was Ramer's third grade teacher Jeanette Winetsky reading the class Edgar Allan Poe's poem "The Bells" that changed forever the life of the class artist. He'd never heard anyone use words and sound that way, went home, wrote his first poem, and has been writing ever since, having had an experience like the one Emily Dickinson described: "If I feel physically as if the top of my head were taken off, I know that is poetry." Only Ramer felt as if fireworks were shooting up from his heart and out the top of his head!

In 1968 his mother remarried and moved with her sons to California, and he graduated from U.C. Berkeley in 1973 with a degree in Religious Studies, which is where he came out as gay. A year later he and his first boyfriend broke up and he moved back to New York. He worked for several years in book stores in Brooklyn (where he met Lynne Reynolds) Boston and Manhattan. His first published book was *little pictures,* the stories and drawing for which he began working on in college. It was edited by Chris Cox and published in 1987. He was working on *Twenty-two Views of a Life,* an autobiography told through objects, when Cox died, but it's never been published. Nor have the five sequels to *little pictures,* the last of which, *Music of the Spheres,* includes a Ramer family tree that begins with his birth in 1951 and ends in 2571

In 1994 Ramer moved back to California with a former partner. While he now goes by the name Eli, he still writes under the name Andrew. In 2012 he was ordained a maggid, a sacred storyteller in the Jewish tradition. His brother Richard is a gifted pianist and recognized green architect.

Eli Andrew Ramer still paints, draws, and makes small sculptures from found objects. He plays the didgeridoo, only listens to music on CDs—and has more Bach and Billie Holiday than anyone else. Single, he continues to wonder if the story of his own life will be rewritten. And hopes that the retelling of these writers' lives will ripple out into a retelling of the story of how we live on this planet. Think: trees, forests, jungles, and the continuation of life for them and all the beings who live here.

For more information on Ramer's work please visit—www. andrewramer. com

Gratitude

THIS LITTLE BOOK EXISTS as you just read it—because of the wonderful suggestions of the friends who read its first incarnation: Jim Van Buskirk, Sheri Hostetler, Shoshana Levenberg, Beth Piatote, Harvey Schwartz, and Steve Zipperstein. And because of the comments and suggestions of the readers of its several reincarnations: Randy Higgins, Nancy Meyer, Martha Clark Scala, Andrew Lawler, Karen Schiller, Harriet Rafter, Joan Larkin, Eileen Ansel, Eileen Gordon, Michael Starkman, Laura Paull, Erik Gleibermann, Sue Levi Elwell, Edward Myers, Tamara Eskenazi, Mary Feller, Gordon Feller, Mary Jane Eisenberg, Alyson Belcher, Vanessa Kauffman, Justus Zimmerly, and Cheryl Woodruff.

With deep gratitude to my various muses, embodied and disembodied, with and without wings, and to everyone at Wipf and Stock who worked on this book:

Emily Callihan, Assistant Managing Editor

George Callihan, Editorial Administrative Assistant

Shannon Carter, Cover Designer

EJ Davila. Endorsements Manager

Rachel Saunders, Typesetter

Matt Wimer, Managing Editor

The collage on the cover was created by noted artist Lisa Occhipinti and appears with many others in her book *An Annotated Awakening*, in which she illustrates and annotates the early feminist classic *The Awakening* by Kate Chopin, first published in 1899. For information on Lisa and her work, and to order her book, go to: locchipinti.com/

For another example of a retelling of the lives of famous people in history, go to YouTube and watch the short video "Imagine a World Without Hate" from the Anti-Defamation League.